Realm

Turkey
Roost

Pitrin's
Land

an's
ouse

Cedar
Grove

Field of
Dancy

Man's
Road

Murder
Tree

Stream

Quail
Nest

The Land of Lupus Rex

Other books by John Carter Cash

Anchored in Love
Momma Loves Her Little Son
Daddy Loves His Little Girl
House of Cash
The Cat in the Rhinestone Suit

Lupus Rex

John Carter Cash

First published 2013 by Ravenstone
an imprint of Rebellion Publishing Ltd,
Riverside House, Osney Mead,
Oxford, OX2 0ES, UK

www.ravenstone.com

US ISBN: 978 1 78108 114 3
UK ISBN: 978 1 78108 115 0

10 9 8 7 6 5 4 3 2 1

A CIP catalogue record for this book is available from the British Library.

Designed & typeset by Rebellion Publishing
Cover and interior art by Douglas Smith
Map and graphic design by Pye Parr

Printed in the US

To the memory of my father, John R Cash,
who introduced me to the wonders of nature and
the limitless mysteries concealed therein.

A gathering of crows is known as a muster, murder, or storytelling.

Prelude

The Rumor of Doves

THERE WAS A buzz on the line.

That was one reason the doves perched on it. From when they landed until they flew, the buzz filled them as rain does a willow trunk. First tingling their feet, with sharp claws clasped tight to the wire, then up into their bodies and onto the folded tips of their wings, and finally to their heads where it prickled the eager tips of their quills. It felt good.

Then there was the view. From their lofty perch, they could see the Murder's Field, from the south to the north, all of the forest beyond, and the smoky purple-green of the distant peaks as well. They watched from here the goings-on below and paid close attention to where the other birds were gathered. If there was a gathering, there was surely food—maybe grain. That was the first thing they looked for: animals feeding.

On the line they heard news. The wind always brought news to the doves. One would hear and whisper into another's ear, and likewise that one to another. If Zeno were to ask Tropha, "Where did you hear that?" (which he never did), Tropha would say, "I heard it from my brother." And if the brother were to ask the next, "Where did you hear that?" (which he never did), that one would say, "I heard it from my cousin." And if the cousin were asked where he heard it, he would say, "I heard it from . . ." And it would go on until the last of the birds was questioned. He would then reply, "Why, I really don't remember. I am sure Zeno told me." But the birds never asked one another anything at all. There was always too much telling going on. Listening and telling.

And it was on that early fall day, when the first of the stores of grain were being harvested in the field by the man with his machine, and the quail hid and waited for the sun to set low, the time when the man would wipe his brow and drink his cool, brown liquid and go to his house to be fed by his woman, the time when the skunks were sleeping and the captain of the army was seeking the King's child, Nascus, in the north forest, that Zeno whispered the thing to Tropha. And so one to the other and the other to the next and on down the line until they were all cooing softly and excitedly. The doves sat on the line and felt the buzz and cooed and whispered. Then a silence descended, and they looked out upon the forest. Far away and high in the sky, an ebony dot appeared.

The doves sat on the line and felt the buzz.

The dot flattened and took the shape of the crooked end of a broken branch, then shaped to black cutting feathers sifting the air at the ends of furious wings. Another dot appeared behind the winged thing. Crows: the captain of the murder and the middle son of the King. … as grew closer, the doves flew into formatio… …e pyramid—three at the bottom; two, Zeno … Trop…, the middle; and one at the top. Two birds fle… …ust behind the formation, one above the other. And they f… close to the crows, listening for words on the wind or sm…s from scavenging so that they'd have more news to sprea… with what the wind had whispered. But the doves did not f… too close to the General for fear of catching his attention, no… directly behind the crows so as to appear threatening.

And when the dark birds grew close to the King's nest, the doves veered away and flew down to the edges of the field and into the brush to find the quail and the rabbits and the badger and the mice and the rat.

They had news to tell.

Chapter One

Proclamations and Gluttonies

"THE KING IS dead!" cried Jackdaw, flopping his wings in fitful, tumultuous flight. "The time of consideration and, oh, the most fowl grief has come! The King is dead!"

Jackdaw the crier; Jackdaw the jester. He was always joking, always bringing light to the day, even when the snakes woke in spring and the young needed food and there was none. Jackdaw was always cheerful when he was performing his job as crier, but not today. His wings were tired and his throat was dry. He was used to bellowing out, "The spring is here!" Or "Harvest has begun!" (which he had cried the very day before), or even "There is born a new grandchick to the King!" But never in his life had he been required to broadcast such an announcement. These words caused his beak to ache with the effort of driving the phrases through. The wise and brave Mellori was dead. Life was finished as he had known it.

And all the animals in and around the field heard his words. The rabbits huddled in fear. The moles and mice paid little heed, hidden away in their dens, but those who did hear only pushed deeper into their burrows.

Within the tight brush, beyond the border of the field, too thick for a crow to see into, the quail heard the proclamation also. Within his scanty nest, Ysil the quail listened to Jackdaw with waxing interest. *When the leaves are gone, we will be seen from above*, he thought to himself, looking up through the canopy of green. The thought brought on more fear and he looked nervously about him to the other quail, some within their nests, and some moving around and chattering to one another in excitement.

The quail had already heard the news before Jackdaw made his announcement. The doves had all descended into the protective thicket as one. Ysil had never seen this before, and it frightened him. Cotur Ada looked up, his eyes opening wide in apprehension, when Tropha the dove descended with a flutter beside them. Ysil watched for his grandfather's reaction to the dove's arrival to determine his own (*should I fly?*), but Cotur Ada smiled to the dove and offered out his ear to hear its whisper. Ysil's chest swelled with a rush of breath. Each of the doves had gone to an elder quail and whispered into their proffered ears. One dove had settled close to Incanta in her nest. The old quail lay sleepy and limp, her eyes cracking drearily open. Her wings had been broken years before in an escape from a coyote, and she was cared for by all. When the dove whispered his news to the wise old matriarch, her eyes popped wide in shock and she stood up and shook her feathers. The doves all jumped up in one movement, and in a swift flight they were gone, surely to spread the word elsewhere.

Incanta called out, "A rare and sad day it is! The King is dead!" She had not asked Henic where he had heard the news, nor did she question its validity. The doves were never wrong.

Cotur Ada had risen from his nest in a flutter and taken to the sky. With the departure of his grandfather, Ysil had become instantly uneasy. Why had he so swiftly departed? Where had he so hurriedly gone?

Within a matter of moments, the quail became frantic. And though they were by creation cautious and fidgety, frantic was rare.

"The King is dead!" one cried. "A new King will be crowned," whispered another. "What does this mean to us?" The rites of kingship were little known, and no living quail had witnessed them.

"The day a new King takes the throne is a dangerous one," Ysil heard Cotur Mono whisper in the din that came from about the elder's nest. "It is a dangerous one for the two who are not chosen King, but to us also."

"We must let the crows' worries be theirs and not ours," said Ensis.

"We may not have that choice," replied Cotur Mono.

When Jackdaw made his announcement, the quail's nest was still amuck with the uneasiness of the dove's news. But it wasn't long until the concern in their heads was overtaken by a nagging of greater import: hunger in the belly. The field was covered in grain. The smell was everywhere. So the news lost its sting and the crying of the gut took precedent.

It was the time of harvest, the time to save, not splurge (which came with the green of spring). However, these were uncertain times.

So the subject of conversation changed. "Perhaps the crows will forget their order," said one bird. "Even though they always get first pick at the grain, they always leave a good deal for us. This may not be the way with the King dead! They may take it all!"

There came a murmur of agreement.

The man had ridden the bellowing giant the day before and had not yet raked with the spinning giant. The grain was spread out all across the field, its fresh smell enticing and delicious in the air.

From beneath the limber trunk of the hackberry, Ysil watched the first of the quail leave the assumed safety of the nest and scurry in the direction of the beckoning field. Ysil listened to the hop of rabbits' feet and the scurry of mice passing the brush where he sheltered. It seemed a common hunger was calling the other lesser animals also. Hearing a flutter of wings, he looked up to a branch above. It was Cormo, his friend for life. Cormo was Cotur Mono's son's son, and the two had always been side by side, usually nesting together and keeping company most every day. With the courage of hunger urging him on, he jumped on wing to the branch and settled beside Cormo. With little more than a look, they descended in a rush of flight to the edge of the Murder's Field and stood gazing at the bounty of grain. At first, they only looked. In view of the golden grain spread out before them, the news of the King's death lessened in consequence.

The field itself was shaped like a turtle, and though the crows knew it as the Murder's Field, the quail thought of it as simply 'the field'. In the direction where the sun rose, it extended the length of twenty great trees, until it narrowed down to a path, which wound down into the valleys below. To the right and in the middle of the field itself was a small stand of oaks. The greatest and tallest of these was the Murder's Tree, and deepest within the tree, protected by the nests of the others, was the nest of the King. Ysil could see the shapes of many dark birds gathered upon the branches of the Murder's Tree now, all squawking excitedly to one another. In the direction where the sun set, the field extended another twenty great trees' lengths. Just past the tree line, within tangles of thorny bushes, he knew the rabbits watched also, finally away from the assumed safety of their dens. At the northwest corner of the field was the tallest and greatest tree of any Ysil knew: a great old fir, its top broken out in some long-ago storm. Within its uppermost branches, bleached nearly white by the rains, snows, and suns of many seasons, were the uninhabited remains of the hawk Elera's nest.

Ysil saw a shape move into the field with seeming unconcern for safety. It was Roe the rat. Crows be cursed, he would follow his belly's call. Roe was always hungry, and a bit fat. And though he never stopped complaining about his hunger, Ysil had few times seen him when he was not eating.

Mice, badgers, groundhogs, and squirrels gather the grain, and they house it in burrows, but the quail hold equal rights to the stores, for they hold equal space in the field. But it seemed for the while this order had been forgotten. The rule of hunger was taking over now.

Ysil fidgeted, watching the rat eat. His belly growled.

"Dear me!" came a voice they both knew well from behind. "What noise was that? Perhaps a bear about to rise up from the ground?" It was Gomor, the rabbit. He hopped over to his two friends, his floppy ears bouncing in time with his hops. "I am hungry, too," he said. "But keep it down. You don't want to wake the skunks!"

"Hello, Gomor," said Ysil. "What do you think? Perhaps we should eat while we can, eh? Do you think the crows will break order and take all of the grain?"

"I don't know about any of that, but I am starved. I am going to eat." And with that the rabbit hopped off toward the feasting rat.

"Surely there remains order in the tree," said Cormo, though not too hopefully. "But still, we should take advantage of this chance while we still have it." They both fluttered out into the field and began to peck.

Then, even with Jackdaw flying around the field, still delivering his cheerless report, the animals began to come out from everywhere—the mice, the squirrels, then the rabbits, and finally more quail. Roe lowered his head as he fed, his eyes closed. Then with a rush, Jackdaw flew at Roe, barely passing above the rat's head.

"Warning!" sounded the crier.

As Jackdaw passed above, Roe made no sign of concern. He only chewed and chewed.

Ysil ate also. He looked up to see the field full of every animal he knew. But for the old, all of the quail were there, and the rabbits were all steadfastly chewing. Ysil could not remember a time when he had seen all the rabbit family in the same place at the same time, except in their den. Sylvil the quail was even walking the border of the field nervously. For her to be out in the open was rare, and Ysil knew there was no way she would venture into the middle of the field.

Not one of them looked at the other, perhaps knowing that in doing so they would have to hold one another accountable for their anxious feast. Food may be eaten when it is there, but first, the dens are to be filled. And then food may be eaten only after the crows had their fill. This was the order. And since quail did not fill the dens, they were the last to receive their portion.

Ysil saw that Harlequin was with her brothers, Anur and Erdic, eating. She was so dainty and thoughtful with each peck. Then she turned her head toward him and he quickly looked away. It was then that Monroth strutted by, and when Ysil noticed him, so did Harlequin. Monroth made no reservations about looking her right in the eye and waved a wing in greeting. Ysil flushed. Harlequin raised her wing to him in return, then went back to what she was doing. When Ysil looked back to Monroth, the larger quail was smiling at him with a look that said, *She's mine, and you know it.*

Monroth had been hatched the same season as Cormo and Ysil. He was proud and growing more so all the time. He kept his gaze tight in place, the two quail eye to eye. Finally, Ysil lowered his head and returned to his chewing.

"You must all stop your peckings and munchings right now!" came a voice from the left, from the direction of the rabbits' dens. "We must store away before we feast. You all know the law. There must be order!" It was Sulari, the old gray hare. Behind him walked the ample form of Rompus the badger. Cotor Mono, the leader of the quail, landed beside the old hare in a flurry. Sulari was hopping quickly toward the center of the field. He seldom hopped at all, and to see him move with such speed was rare indeed. He was nervous and a bit angry. All eyes turned his way and chewing ceased.

"We are under decree from King Crow. We must follow order!" This time it was Rompus who spoke. The hair around his head and on his back was as white as that under his belly.

"We must eat while we can," came a defiant voice. It was Monroth. *Showing off for Harlequin*, thought Ysil. "If the crows break order they will all be on the field today and the grain will be gone."

"There will be no break in order," said Cotur Mono. He eyed Monroth and sized up the younger quail. "The order has long been established, and the death of the King is within this order. We must all do as the law decrees, set aside our fears and follow the ancient ways. We are never to tie together if we break this chain. Things are as decreed for good reason. Monroth, you are young and full of energy. If only you were as wise as you are eager."

Monroth lowered his head in embarrassment.

"I will eat as I always eat," said the golden rat. He lowered his head. Neither quail, hare, nor badger responded, knowing it would be no use to try to change the scavenger's mind.

All around the field the animals listened and considered, although Erdic and Anur rolled about the grain and laughed, showing not the least concern.

Jackdaw disappeared back into the Murder's Tree, leaving the air above in foretelling stillness. Moments after, with a great whooshing, the Murder's Tree exploded with black winged shapes. The crows descended on the field. Many of the other birds, mice, and rabbits ran for cover, but a good few held fast. Ysil and Cormo both froze in apprehension, too afraid to fly, lest they draw specific attention to themselves. Monroth also froze, and if the look in his eye was of any sign, it was fear that held him and not bravery. A cold chill came to Ysil's heart, and he could feel the wind from the beating of the crow's wings. The gray hare Sulari stood on his hind legs and pitched his ears to the sky as the huge form of Fragit, the crow General, crashed down directly in front of him. The rest of the murder followed, all landing to form a rough circle around the hare, quail, and badger. Ysil, Cormo, and Monroth huddled in closer to the elders. There were also a number of other quail and rabbits within the crows' boundary. Harlequin was there. The lesser animals all fidgeted and hopped nervously about, looking to one another and the crows.

If they were to decide such, they could easily destroy us all, Ysil thought, his feathers standing up as with the smell of lightning. *Should I fly anyway?* But the young quail found no such courage, nor did he see any in his friend Cormo, or from any of the others. The murder moved in, closing up any gaps in the circle. Ysil knew a good number of them by name and reputation, though he had never spoken to the first. Milus, the third-born prince, was there; as was Sintus, who was firstborn. Nascus, the second-born prince, Ysil did not count in the number.

"How dare you eat the grain before the stores are filled! Quail! Rabbits! Mice! It is not in the order!" bellowed Fragit.

Many of the animals cowered, some quail even hiding their heads under their wings. A few rabbits tightened up into small, furry balls, attempting to be invisible. But the old gray hare, Rompus, and Cotur Mono stood their ground. Sulari rose higher on his hind legs and with as much height as he could muster (easily as tall as the mighty crow), looked the General straight in the eye and said, "We will follow order. There were some of our number who grew careless with the news of the King's passing. They grew frightened that your kind would come and clear the fields for your own bellies before we had the chance to get our part. I have assured them the great General Fragit would never allow something of that sort to happen." Sulari eyed him thoughtfully. "That is true, eh, General?"

The General only grew more frustrated and agitated at the mere thought of such a thing. "Sulari, watch your tongue or I may rip it out—a tender morsel to precede dinner! You must be aware that of all times to maintain order, now is that time indeed." With this, the badger, who had been standing beside Sulari, moved to his rear. The hare stood his ground, as did Cotur Mono. Fragit hopped back a step from the three and shook his wings to gather attention. "Now! All hear! Animals watching from the bush and here in the field! Tomorrow there will be the Reckoning! All will clear the field and surrounding bush by tomorrow's quarter sun! None may witness the Reckoning but for crow kind. This is the order!" And with that he hopped another step back and turned, preparing to take to wing.

"Wait, O great and respected General," called Rompus, finding sudden courage and stepping out from behind Sulari's back. Fragit stopped and looked back in annoyance. "If we are to go, it may come rain. Pickings of the best grain we must store this morning, and then the spoils taken later after the man has threshed. If we must leave tomorrow, we will not be able to gather those spoils. The rest could go bad . . . and with all gone, your kind, O mighty General, will be the only to seek the har—"

A quickened pounding of black feathers cut off the badger's voice. In a fury, Fragit was on the badger, pecking at his head and shoulders. Rompus succumbed and lay still. Even though he was a good bit larger than the General and could surely manage to free himself from Fragit's grasp, he would then face the whole of the murder. Against such great number he stood no chance. So he lay prone while the General flogged and pecked, the blood flowing from his brow and into his eyes. The violent assault passed, and General Fragit hopped away. All around them the murder cawed in boisterous approval.

"Do not question! It is not for the lesser animals to question!" He raged thus and pounded his wings. "You will gather for the stores today, all that you can! The Reckoning must commence tomorrow!" He took to wing, and the rest of the crows rose with him as of one mind. "It is the order!" he cried out as they flew up and into the Murder's Tree.

Rompus lay in a frazzled heap in the middle of the field; undeniably the crows' field. Sulari moved to his side and laid his warm form next to the badger, offering solace and comfort. The badger looked to his friend. "I never know when to be quiet, do I?" he asked feebly. Ysil could see that there were a number of cuts on Rompus's head and not a few on his shoulders, but that he was not greatly harmed, only bruised and humiliated.

"We must speak when our hearts command," said Cotur Mono, stepping to the hare and badger. "You are guilty only of that. Now, we must gather grain while there is time. The hour is near when the man will come."

With a somewhat difficult effort, Rompus rose to his feet and waddled away. At the edges of the field, the squirrels, chipmunks, mice, and a few rats were scampering about eagerly, gathering grain in their mouths and running back into the brush. Within seconds they would return, gather more, and rush back into the bushes.

"My dear friends," called the old gray hare, "make great haste! The gathering time is here. Make great haste!" He hopped away to join the effort with the rest of the gatherers.

With that the quail and the doves flew into the brush. All was in chaos within the nesting bush. Harlequin was beside her brothers, helping to feed Incanta, her old feeble form bent low. Monroth was close to the old one. As he passed, Ysil heard Monroth say, "Don't worry, Grandmother. I will protect Harlequin and the little ones. The journey will not be hard." Incanta looked up to the young quail with a minor curiosity.

Ysil was disgusted. "Let's go, Cormo," he said.

As they passed, Ysil heard the old quail answer Monroth. "You will, will you? I am sure there are many who will be looking after you, young one."

They walked through the bustle of the nest and past its border into the open woods beyond. There was a small clearing behind the first row of bramble bush, and Ysil made his way to that more private spot. Gomor was there, as was Sylvil.

"Look what I found!" said Gomor, and there beneath him was a small pile of blackberries, ripe and tasty. The four of them sat in the clearing and ate, talking of the morning and what was to come the next day. Gomor would soon have to go back to help gather and fill the burrow, but seemed to have slipped the duty for now. Sylvil was quiet as usual, but naturally gravitated to Cormo.

Cormo looked to Ysil. "What is the Reckoning?" he asked.

"I don't know," answered Ysil. "But within the whispering of the elders this morning I heard Cotur Mono speaking to Monroth. He asked Mono if he knew when there would be a new King Crow. Cotur Mono said 'After the Reckoning.' Exactly what this ceremony is, none of us know for sure—certainly a fearful thing!"

Gomor looked confused. "But why wouldn't Sintus be the new King? He's the oldest."

"I don't know, and I don't think any of us ever will. We won't be here."

"Oh! Yes and hurray!" said Gomor with newfound enthusiasm. "Just what I always wanted to do—take a journey with my best friends! A high adventure is upon us!"

"A dangerous adventure, certainly," said Cormo.

The rabbit's face dropped. "Oh, yes, I do suppose so," Gomor said, his sudden excitement abated.

Then they heard the man's machine come to life far away and to the west. It would not be long now until his thrashing began. Ysil prayed the animals had enough time to gather before the man's arrival. So Gomor left to return to his burrow, and the three quail returned to their bramble.

When they entered the nest it seemed the commotion had not settled in the least; rather, it had most certainly grown.

"I will not go," spoke Incanta defiantly but softly. "I am old and there is no need. The crows will not even know I am here. What's one old quail to them? I am simply not up to making such a trip. And besides, when we are all walking and a couple of coyotes jump us, everyone will fly, everyone except me, that is, as I cannot. I will be their dinner then, and a meager one at that!"

Cotur Ada had returned by then, with no word of where he had been. "You must succumb to the crows' order, Incanta," he said gently. "It is within their specific order that we all depart here together."

"Well, it is my specific order that I stay," she answered, a spry light in her wrinkled eyes.

There was much consideration and argument, but finally the covey allowed that she would remain behind. Ysil heard the sound of the man's machine getting closer now. The man would work all day, gathering the grain. The old bird sat back down in her nest and closed her eyes. As Ysil passed her she mumbled under her breath: "Damned crows . . ."

Chapter Two

Travels and Hastened Returns

THE MORNING WAS hot as the band of animals set out for the Vulture Field, also known as "Olffey Field." Just the thought of the terrible place cast a pall over Ysil.

Ysil and Cormo moved past Sulari in a single-file line as the old hare counted each and every animal under his care.

When the count was done, the group separated into smaller groups of their own kind. Sulari hopped up to Cotur Mono and gave his count: "There are twenty-nine quail, fifty-five mice, twenty-two rabbits, fourteen squirrels, five badgers, and one slow, grumbling golden rat," he said. "And I the only hare."

"Ahem," said Cotur Mono. "My count is also the same."

"Now, on!" said the hare, rising up to his tallest. "On with you all! We must away." And with his word the group departed the wooded vale next to the field.

"The vultures," said Cormo, keeping in pace with his friend. "Why are we going to the vultures?"

"The elders say there is safety there," said Ysil.

"Safety," snorted Cormo. "As safe as death, I suppose."

The vultures were peaceful by nature. They just waited patiently for the food that would surely come. Ysil had heard tales of young rogue vultures who were liable to kill small animals, but the mother vulture, Ekbeth, in her field at least, demanded control. A slow-moving group of rabbits, mice, and quail could reach Olffey Field in a full day's walk.

Ysil strode along thoughtfully and watchfully between the trunks of the yellow birches and mossy-cup oaks. The group passed scattered piles of bottlebrush buckeyes, which they left alone. Buckeyes were far too tough-skinned for a quail to break open, and even if they could, the bitter meat therein would cause pain in the stomach. He stayed as close as he could to the middle of the covey, feeling safest there.

The animals formed a rough symmetry. On the outside of the circle were the stronger quail, while within the circle were the younger quail and the elder. Sylvil was in the exact center, quiet and nervous. Ysil walked close to Cotur Ada, watching his grandfather's every move. Ysil truly enjoyed being close to Cotur Ada, and though the young bird loved to hear his grandfather speak, the elder was often with little to say.

Ysil was fascinated with his grandfather. He thought of the scar on Cotur Ada's side, the missing toe on his right foot. How had these things happened? Ysil had not yet summoned the nerve to ask these questions. Would he ever?

"You know, when I was a young bird, we would not venture far unless there were many birds in distinct form. Now, I am sure you and your friends walk fearlessly, even far into the woods. But you should be wary, ever cautious.

Everything that eats meat eats quail, and man certainly hunts with his booming stick." The elder quail submitted these careful suggestions often. Ysil took heed, certainly, but he had heard this same speech the week before, when he and Gomor had gone to see the mice in their harvest dance. The crazy little things still danced every year, though it had been rumored that Strix—with his sharp talons and giant eyes—had been ranging near again. But it was hard to tell whether the field mice were losing numbers as their memories were so short. It seemed they remembered only the good things—where the food was, for instance, and, of course, when the summer moon's dance should occur.

"Grandfather, tell me of when the hawk still nested in the great fir." This was, in fact, one of the questions Ysil had wished to ask Cotur Ada for a long time, and his sudden audacity had come with the ensuing excitement of travel. Had the circumstance not been as it was, and he was simply living another day in search of food and milling about the nest, he most certainly would have never asked this. But there it was: the question. He always felt it strange that the quail had nested so near the hawk, but he knew it was because of the 'order' and the rule of crows. He also knew that the rule of crows would not govern the hawk, nor the vulture for that matter, but still neither birds of prey nor carrion ruled the crows. No one did; only their order governed. Even King Crow succumbed to it.

The old bird looked at him with trepidation and a barely disguised annoyance. But then Cotur Ada smiled and touched his wing to Ysil's. "The hawk was vicious and proud. She was strong, but in the end, foolish. We all feared her, and many, old and young, were lost. Few mourned her passing."

The old quail looked forward, and Ysil could tell he did not intend to go any further with his recollection.

But the young bird would not be put off. "But she was a mother hawk. I heard Incanta say that once. Not just female, but a mother. What happened to her young? Where are they? The young vultures stay with their family, as do the crows and robins. Don't hawks?"

"No, they do not," said Ada. "Once the hawks learn to fly, they are gone. They range until they claim a territory, then they nest for life."

"Did Elera have chicks that flew before she died?" Ysil was getting brave in his questioning. He noticed that Cormo was staying close and listening. Monroth was staying to the outside of the circle, but he looked at them occasionally. He seemed to be listening also.

Cotur Ada thought for a moment then, smiling, he responded. "No," he said and was quiet for a brief moment. "None flew before she died. Now, I would rather you not mention her name, if you wish to please me."

Ysil walked along, his mind racing. He held his tongue as long as he could. Finally he had to ask. "Well, where is the nearest occupied hawk's nest?"

Ada looked down at Ysil. He was quiet for a bit, and Ysil thought he might not respond. "Toward the rising sun, past the lines and through the forest, past the Belasyvis Hills and dangerously near the Sugar Valley of men, beyond shadowy stands of hemlocks where the toothworts and rock brakes grow thick. Then down a steep trail. The journey is less than two days walking, and perhaps less than a day if you fly. At the end of the trail there is a wide river. On the far side of that river is the territory of the hawk Pitrin. It is a journey you never need make, and really, I do not know why I tell you the path. Pitrin is the child of Elera."

Ysil was confused. "But you said she didn't have fledglings that flew before she died." He looked to his grandfather but could not read his expression.

"The chick did not learn to fly until after she died," said Cotur Ada.

Ysil said, "But how could it have survived, in the nest not flying and with its mother dead? How did it eat?"

Ada laughed a little and brushed Ysil on the brow feathers. "We have talked enough about hawks now. You need not worry about them at all. Pitrin has vowed to never return here. And should he make an attempt after such a long absence, the crows would drive him out, as they would any hawk. Of course, they hold no power over the larger bird, but the hawk does follow an order: its own. Now, this talking has worn a poor old bird out greater than this forced trudge we are set upon. Quiet, young one."

In frustration Ysil snapped closed his gaping beak. He looked to Cormo, who, having heard every word, walked along dazed. The other birds' eyes were full of wonder.

THE ANIMALS CONTINUED on through the middle of the day until they reached a small clearing that held a good stand of clover. The clearing was encircled with a thick brush of blackberries, and the fruit was ripe. The wind was soft and steady, and the area held no scent of predator, so the group set to feeding on the greenery and the seed it held. The quail fed for a while, their heads down. It was evident that few deer or turkey had found the clearing, for it was bountiful, and the birds and furred ate as much as they desired, but not so much as to become heavy.

"All together now!" called Sulari, who had been conversing with Cotur Mono and Gomor. It was not so much a conversation as a scolding of the two upon Gomor. The rabbit had wandered off for a time in open hardwoods. Anywhere alone without cover was no place for a rabbit, the old hare had told him.

"Anur and Erdic! Where are you?" It was Nova. She was mother to the two and also Harlequin. Immediately the quail set to searching, flying about, and conferring with one another about the possible location of the two chicks. The mother searched, but the two were nowhere to be found. When the mother quail sat down, her head beneath her wing, and began to cry, Ensis stepped forth.

"I heard them talking earlier," said Ensis, Cormo's grandfather and mate to Incanta, though he was somewhat younger than her. "They said, 'We should go back to the field. We can hide and the crows will never see us.' Anur said he knew the perfect place to watch and not be seen. I didn't think much of it when I heard them, just thought it to be the chatter of chicks, if you please, but sadly I was mistaken."

Though Cotur Ada was the eldest, he was not the leader. Cotur Mono held that distinction, if it could be truly said there was a leader of the quail. He talked for a while with Sulari, and it was decided that an elder quail and two younger would go back to search out the chicks. Monroth was the first to volunteer.

"I will go," said Monroth with a righteous tone. "I will bring them back well before sunset. They could not have gotten far."

"You are eager, young one," said Sulari. "Mayhap your eagerness will set you up in a coyote's belly. You may go, but certainly not alone."

"I will go." It was Cotur Ada.

In response the group stared at him, all eyes wide and unblinking. Then Rompus spoke: "Wise One, you are strong and respected, but you're not expected to venture on such a mission. You're more needed here, as our guide."

"Oh, you are smart in the way of the tongue, badger, and certainly I am flattered, but there stands a point: the chicks need to be taught a lesson, and I will be the one to teach it. Now, I will take one more volunteer." To this the badger held his response. "As far as being your guide, you need only to follow the trail. Cotur Mono knows it as well as I."

"I will go," said Ysil, and none disagreed.

So it was decided that the three would go in search of the young ones. Harlequin wanted to go as well and insisted that it was her responsibility to watch after the chicks, feeling it her lack of attention that had allowed them to escape notice during their departure. Certainly, Monroth and Ysil both would have enjoyed her company, even if it was just to look upon her, but alas, her joining them was denied by Cotur Mono, who insisted no more of the group be disbanded.

Harlequin looked to the two younger sojourners. "Be careful, you two. I will miss you both."

A lump came into Ysil's throat and he stumbled for something to say in return. Before he could manage a word, Monroth quipped, "Don't worry, little one. I will be fine, of course. And not to worry a bit about these other two. I will be taking care of them."

Ysil nearly spat up the clover he had half digested.

So as the majority of animals set off for the Vulture Field, three quail returned down the woodland trail and back toward their home in search of the irresponsible small ones.

Within the darkness of the thick brush surrounding, there were four eyes watching the scene with intense interest. And when the three were a good distance from their separated, there was a slight rustling of limbs and leaf, and two sleek, furry shapes carefully and silently pursued the smaller group.

THE WIND ALWAYS whistles to a quail's ear. The sounds of the forest are always beneath the ever-present harmony of whistles. When the wind dies, the birdsong and animal sounds become no more apparent and no louder to the quail, as the wind does not stifle the forest's noise but enhances it. Nature's sounds are much like music to the quail, with the wind being the rhythm. In this way, quail need not speak of the sound of an approaching storm or the approach of a predator, or for that matter the arrival of a crow. These things are like a new voice or instrument being added to a song. And though quail are careful and cautious, they often offer their song to the music of nature.

As they set upon their way, the three joined in song. Perhaps to a man's ear the song would have seemed an unharmonious chirping with the occasional shrill note added in randomly. But to the quail it was the song of their lives.

They sang:

When winter's rain is hardened cold
By winds from north and high

We will not hunger days untold
Nor weep for bleeding sky

We'll eat the finest golden grain
Among the sanctified
In that field beyond the darkened door
Past life's fast burned light.

Around our mother's welc'ming nest
We'll gather safe and warm
Beneath her gentle wings we'll rest
Forever free from harm

In that field beyond the darkened door
With no future and no past
In that field beyond the darkened door
We'll know the truth at last.

And though the words of the song were sad, Ysil felt happy as he sang. He couldn't remember a time when he did not know the words and melody. It was sung in small gatherings and when the covey held full council. It was the Quailsong, and all quail knew it. It was the song of travel and it was the song of home. It was sacred to them, and for another animal to sing it would hold no purpose. The other animals had their own songs.

But that day as the song died within the beaks there was only a moment of silence. Then there came a mocking murmur from the surrounding brush, and the melody that joined in with the wind was a whispered and vile voice. It was a voice Cotur Ada had heard before and one Monroth knew well (though he did not yet speak such), but Ysil did not. The melody was the same as the Quailsong, but the words were changed, and the harmony it brought was one broken and without amity. The birds, poised for flight, froze when they heard the voices:

Quailsies reach the darkened door
For foxes we will bite,
Quailsies they will fly no more
In foxes' teeth so tight.

With a flurry the bushes burst and out jumped two foxes. In the same moment the quail flew. In a breath's time, Ysil realized that the foxes had not intended to kill them, at least not yet, but only to scare them. However, at that moment Ysil felt the fear of death, and he forced its power beneath his wings. The quail perched in a shellbark hickory above, leaving the foxes below. The two on the ground burst into triumphant laughter at the quails' terrified flight.

"Quailsies need not fear!" cried the larger of the two. "We only wanted to scare you! That we did, eh?"

To Ysil's amazement Monroth responded to the two by name. "Drac and Puk, you did not scare me! I will stab a sharpened beak in your eyes should your teeth get close!"

Cotur Ada looked to Monroth. "We do not speak to furred red ones, chick; this you know. They are troublesome and cunning. We should fly far now, out of reach. Come, young ones."

But Monroth reacted as if he had not heard the elder. "I will come down there and pierce your bellies with my talons! I have sharpened them, and they are as fearful as an eagle's!"

The two below laughed heartily. "And you, birdie, *should* come down. We mean you no harm and have no intention to fight. We eat micies, yes, but no quail. Foxes eat fishes and bugs, but no quail. Quail are too pretty and foxes like to look at them. We only joke with you. Foxes want to be friends . . ."

"Do not listen to them, chicks," said Cotur Ada. "You can never trust a fox. They will act as friends until you are close, then when you show them your back, the fox will turn and eat you. A fox will think of only one thing when its belly is empty."

"Monroth, don't talk to them! They can't be trusted," said Ysil.

"Oh, you both are so out of the times. These are trustworthy foxes. I spoke to Drac and Puk last moon. We scavenged late in the back field, and they were there. Tried to scare us, but didn't try to hurt us. I talked to Drac for a long time. As a matter of fact, I like him."

"He is a killer of animals, and were he the sweetest of all foxes, he could not turn against his nature. That is his order. You must follow your own."

To Ysil, his grandfather's words were those of wisdom, but Monroth only laughed and called down to the foxes, "I will come down now and show these old ones we're respectable to each other! What say, boys?" And before the wise elder could protest, Monroth flew down and with a flurry settled on Drac's back. "Let's go for a ride, Drac! Like we did midsummer!" The two ran around the clearing like childhood playmates, laughing as they went.

"This is not safe," called Cotur Ada. "Do not go near the sharp teeth!"

"Fly quick," called Ysil. "He will bite you!"

Monroth paid them no heed and continued his ride. He hooted and whistled as the fox ran around the clearing. Then the fox took off out of the clearing and disappeared into the overgrowth, a thick tangle of mountain laurel and lobelia. For a few minutes there was no sign of them but for a continued rustling of the bushes. Ysil began to feel certain that the fox had turned on Monroth and eaten him. Puk, the older of the two, had stayed within the clearing and continued to laugh. He began again his mocking song. Ysil noticed that Cotur Ada did not even look at the fox but kept his eyes focused on the spot where Monroth and Drac had disappeared. After what seemed much too long, the fox came dancing back into the clearing and still perched on his back, like some miniature winged horseman, was the young adventuresome quail.

"Ha-ha," cried Monroth. "Every quail needs a fox to ride! Maybe this is the way it is meant to be!"

"Monroth," commanded Cotur Ada—and this time there was something passionately consuming about his tone, "get off that fox now and come back up here."

The young quail looked up to the elder and seemed to hear him for the first time. "Oh, all right," relented Monroth. "You're no fun at all, old bird." And with that he flew from the fox's back and up into the tree. He landed on the branch beside Cotur Ada and looked at Ysil, who eyed him incredulously. "What?" he asked. "What's the worry? I told you, I have known these foxes for a while. They are harmless."

"As I said, chick, there is no safe relationship between quail and fox," said Cotur Ada. "Pray you learn this easily before the harder way. When I was but a few moons older than you, Monroth, a fox killed my father." This he said with hushed tones. Then the wise quail looked down to the foxes. "What do you want, tricksters? Why are you here?"

It was Puk that answered. "We only watch as so many animals go by and wonder: *What could all the animals be traveling together for, and in such haste?* And Drac says, 'Must be the crows sent them moving.' And I says to meself: *What could the crows be sending the animals away for?* And then I remembers! Me old father tell me when I's a pup 'bout the way of the crows, how when the King dies, them big black birds make all the other animals leave so as they have the field all to theirselves. And then it hits me: The King is dead! The old King Crow is gone! And there's much to do now, if you're a fox. Much to do."

"Surely, you have guessed correctly. The King is dead," said Cotur Ada. "Now, go on your way and let me and these two continue our journey."

"Oh, joy of a lifetime! The King is dead!" Puk ran in circles around the tree the quail were perched in. "Did you hear that, Drac? Most certainly I was right! The King is dead! The time of the fox is coming soon, for certain!"

Ysil looked to Cotur Ada. "What does he mean?" he asked.

"I am afraid he is hoping the day is near when the foxes may go to the field and pillage the mice nests," answered Cotur Ada. "The King Crow kept them safe. But there will be the same wisdom and protection from the next King. He is forgetting that."

And Drac joined Puk in his celebration, hopping and bouncing around the tree. Ysil, at Cotur Ada's side, with Monroth also looking on, watched the dangerous animals below with a grotesque fascination.

It was not long before the foxes gave up their celebration and ran off to the deeper woods. When they did leave, the quail waited a good ten minutes before flying down to the trail.

Cotur Ada had chastened Monroth for his irresponsible behavior while in the hickory tree, and once they were on the ground it did not stop. And even though Monroth eventually conceded and told the old bird that his word was wise and admitted he had been foolish, Ysil believed that Monroth really did not mean it. He thought there was a message to be found in his cousin quail's eye. It was a look of prideful knowledge, as if his mind were made up no matter what his tongue professed. Ysil knew that Monroth wanted to be friends with the foxes, the old bird be damned.

The trail widened and the quail, without thinking about it, moved to the edges of the brush, out of view of the clear sky. From the open sky death did often descend.

The old bird went on admonishing Monroth as they walked, then he set his eyes on both of the young quail with fiercesome warning. "But even the foxes aside," said Cotur Ada, "the truly foolish thing would be to show yourselves to the crows while in their Reckoning. They will not play with you and use you to their needs, as the wily red ones do. You both need to be full aware of the danger of our mission. The crows will open your hot bodies and share your blood. Then they will leave your feathers to blow in the wind, your bones to dry in the sun. I pray we find the young ones before we reach the field, for if the crows have found them, they are already dead."

Ysil shook involuntarily at the elder's words, the imagery quite effective. Monroth betrayed nothing, his countenance unfazed.

The path came into a dale where Ysil had played many times. They were not far from the nest now, dangerously close to the field. Then they heard it. The cawing screeches of the murder. The jagged cacophony of sound cut through the forest and left Ysil trembling. He had never heard this before, though many times he had heard various murder songs. Sometimes they cawed for no evident reason at all, but today the song was a chaotic melody of screeches, notes, and words. None of the crows' cries were understandable. And even with their cawing as loud as it was, there was no sense to be made of it.

"We must get a quick look at the field from the thickness of the hemlock above, only a quick look to see if the little ones are there," said the old quail, "then we must take to the undergrowth and remain within no matter what we see or hear."

The birds flew to the top of the hemlock and from there could barely see the field. Scattered all across their distant home were many small black spots. More crows gathered in one spot than Ysil had ever seen. From what they could discern at such a distance there were no quail within the field, alive or dead, and Ysil was relieved. Then they flew to the forest floor once again, and peeking into every bush and beneath each stump, made their way along the trail, occasionally calling a low trill for the immature and unwise birds.

Chapter Three

The Reckoning

The King is dead!
We must ahead
The words be read
By magic head.

The King is gone
We join in song
The King is gone
We loved him long!

THE CROW SONG'S words of celebration were cast within the screeching chorus that ruled the field. Some sang this over and over, but many more were merely making noise. The crows made their great gathering known to any who might come near, the tumult of their cawing and screeching so loud as to still even the songs of the mockingbirds and the jays, who kept a good distance. None but Ophrei and

Fragit even knew what the Reckoning would entail, but there was enough knowledge to spread rumored suspicion. The field's grain had been cleared by the man's machine, and the birds knew the man would not likely venture this far from his home again until the spring, so they cawed in unabated excitement. A crow seldom tries not to be heard, for that matter. A crow always draws attention to itself. That is its way.

Jackdaw was back to his eager and excitably happy self again and was hopping around the field, leading the song. The King was dead, and the time for the new one to be chosen had come. This was the Reckoning.

But not all in the field were jovial. The King's three sons were somber and still, each keeping to their own group of followers and family. The three crows' reasons for worry were some the same, but also different.

Nascus, the second-born, had loved the old crow and cried into the wind all the way back to the field. He was afraid of the Reckoning, as all his brothers were, but at the same time knew it must be done. He had known this all his life and accepted it as the order long ago.

On becoming King, Nascus would take the crown and rule—should the Reckoning choose him. The year before, a raging coyote had attacked his mother in the night, its mouth full of foam, its eyes bleeding red. The animal had been driven away, but not before it had taken the life of his gentle mother. Today, Nascus felt the consuming sadness of an orphan, as if the whole of himself had been cut into pieces. He had loved both his parents deeply.

Milus stood in the middle of a small group who held allegiance to him. He was the largest of the three brothers, and the youngest. He was silent and downcast. Milus had always been thoughtful and distant. Nascus watched his brother, and his sadness deepened even more. He knew his younger brother had always dreamed of leaving the field, of beginning a new life. Milus could be given the crown to the Murder's Tree that very day, but his heart was not one of a King and held no dream of becoming one. He loved the wind and the rain, the jagged view of the moon through a white poplar's branches. But though Milus often considered leaving and had even voiced this on occasion to Nascus, he seldom left the field, nor went far from his mother, Edith.

Of the three brothers, Sintus had the dominant group of followers, and they congregated around him. Nascus watched them whisper to him. "You are the wisest!" they were saying, and, "Today you will take your rightful nest!" Sintus was silent and thoughtful, and Nascus knew his brother considered it his destiny to be chosen. He had said so many times to Nascus, and it was no secret to anyone. When the brothers had gathered over their father's lifeless form, Sintus had professed no faith in the Reckoning or in its outcome. The middle brother examined his older sibling's cool and devious eyes that fall afternoon. Today Sintus seemed so certain of himself, his band of followers whispering and cawing in his ear their support. He looked up and caught Nascus's eyes upon him and glared back in disdain and contempt. *You were born of folly and will die a fool's death*, his eyes said.

The largest group of crows held allegiance to General Fragit, which is to say all the rest of the crows, numbering fifty-nine. Within the group was the Guard, twelve crows, strong and mature, dedicated to his command to death.

Beyond these there were no formations to his army, or at least none visible, but the ranks were well known. The General answered to no one on the field now that the King was dead, but he did have an equal. That equal was the rook Ophrei.

Ophrei was the listener, the sorcerer. He heard the whispers of the wind, and at night, while the rest of the crows slept, he spoke to the ghosts. Ophrei was enormously old, older, in fact, than the King would have been had he still lived. No bird remembered a time when Ophrei did not hold council with the King daily. He was the commanding sage and the instructor. Only he knew the way of the Reckoning. This was the order of the crows, that this cousin bird control the ceremony. A crow may hold spoken or unspoken loyalty to animals of other kinds, but a rook held allegiance to none, not even their own. The only fidelity the rook held to was to the wind, and to the order.

When Ophrei stepped out of the circle and moved toward its middle, heading to the center of the field, the singing and cawing descended quickly to a rustling quiet. He hopped and flapped his way slowly until he was encircled by the murder.

"This is the order! All hear," he cried. Jackdaw, who had up to this point been inciting celebration, silenced immediately, the last words of the song echoing with the proclamation from the rook.

"The time of Reckoning has come!" called Ophrei, raising his wings into the air. And as suddenly as their silence had settled, the birds burst into chaotic applause and screeching.

Ophrei quieted them with a lift of his wings. "I require all, prince and soldier alike, to follow my exact order during this Reckoning. This is the order: You will abide by the call and do as led. The General will guide when needed. All birds will respond immediately. Now," he said, "I command a word from each and every one of you, all except the brother princes. Their words I will hear later. But from each of you now I command a word of life. These words are the beginning of the Reckoning, and with it, I will hear the steps." He walked to the edge of the circle and glared at the General. "Fragit will be first."

Fragit looked to the rook, and though it was clear he did not truly understand, he put forward a word. "War," he said.

The rook made no response but went on to the next in the circle. The crow said, "Tomorrow." The next said, "Mouse," and the next, "Forget."

This took a long time for the rook to go around the whole of the field, taking a word from every crow. When he had finished, he walked back to the center of the field, the middle of the circle. The rook sat down in the field and closed his eyes, still now, with the words filling his head like a tall cloud carrying a storm.

"I will now listen to the wind," he said. "The words were within your bodies and beneath your feathers and from your very beaks, crows, but also from the breath of the wind." As he sat he repeated the words the murder had given aloud, occasionally pausing and tilting his ear to the sky as if listening. Finally, he raised his aged head. "The wind has whistled and laid out the path of the Reckoning. In this I have heard the order," said the rook. "General, with you I must hold council."

Fragit walked to the old bird and the two talked for a while, keeping their voices low, so that none other could hear their words. Then, with a determined strut, the general returned to the edge of the circle. He looked to the brothers. "Princes," he called, "you must go to the rook now. The Reckoning has begun."

And when the words of the General reached his ears, Nascus felt a nip of fear strike his belly like the stinger of an enraged wasp.

THE QUAIL DID not go to the nest, as they felt certain the little ones would not be there. Instead they moved through the thickest of the brush, always wary and careful. Cotur Ada felt that every crow in the murder would be in the field, with none patrolling the surrounding woods, but he knew they could not be too careful. Their very lives depended on taking absolute precaution.

They had found no sign of the two young birds. They passed an old groundhog's den and Ysil peered inside, whispering, "Erdic! Anur! Are you there?" but there was no response. Monroth chanced a swift flight up into an old oak where in a rotted hole the two often played, but they were not within. Cotur Ada felt he knew where the two were: hiding on the edge of the field, beneath and within the dull green of the stinging nettle. Why come so far and not be watching the crows? And though the black birds were certainly consumed with their Reckoning, they were always wary and would be watchful for any intruder. They checked each hiding spot they knew of just to be sure.

The nearer to the field they came, the more Ysil's anxiety grew. With each careful step they grew closer and closer to enormous danger. The crows in the field had grown perplexingly silent. The three quail scurried beneath a blackberry bramble, and, shifting their bodies between and beneath the thorny branches and browning leaves, they moved forward until the Murder's Field came into view. Cotur Ada motioned for the two to be silent and still. The quail lay prone within the recess of the bush and observed, listening intently for any sign of the two young birds they were seeking.

IN THE FIELD, the King's sons hopped toward the middle of the circle. The crows in the vast ring were fatally silent as the three approached the old rook.

"This is the order," called Ophrei. Then he turned and stared intensely at the three princes. "You are birds of strength and, to an extent, all rightful by birth. You are the entire one, and still none of you are the whole without the other. One of you will remain in flesh, and the other two will offer their own so that it may become something else." He came close to Sintus, who tendered back an apprehensive eye. "I am the voice and you are the motion. I give form to your word and will hear the telling of the order on the wind. Now, a word of face to each of you. This word is to mirror my own, as your reflection in the still water. Listen carefully and take heed before you speak the word given to you. Listen to it in your heart before you move your tongue." Then he moved his beak to within striking distance of Sintus. "Elder one, you will respond to my word of face with your own. Then, in turn, the other two. This word will determine the order of the Reckoning. Your word is *take*."

Sintus made a slight chuckle under his breath and kept his eyes on his supporters. “Wheat,” he said. Ophrei gazed into his eyes for what seemed a long time but was only a brief moment. The rook moved on to Milus.

“Your word is *remove*,” said the rook to the youngest bird. To this Milus responded after some deliberation, “Storm.” And he broke into a fast breathing, his eyes darting around the field in disquiet.

Then it was the turn for Nascus to offer his word. The rook came close to him, a mirror of sparkle between the two birds’ eyes. “The words will tell the order and the words only,” said the rook, seemingly to no one in particular, though he did not look away from Nascus’s eyes.

“I will claim no preferred,” the rook continued. “Though your tears for your father hold a strong message.” Nascus had noted the other brothers had not cried at all. He did not divert his gaze from that of the rook’s and presented no claim or answer. The rook did not seem to require one. “However,” said the rook, still in his low and measured tone, “I will not allow any acumen to guide the Reckoning.”

Ophrei puffed up and seemed to return to his purpose. “And now, your word of order: *change*,” he said.

With what was the slightest hesitation, but not looking away, Nascus replied: “Fire.”

The old bird looked into Nascus’s eyes for some time. The field around was quiet and still, only a gentle breeze made the slightest sound as it moved through the surrounding trees.

The rook stepped back from the brothers and looked to the surrounding murder. He raised his beak up and called out loudly, the sound of his call piercing the autumnal sky with the certainty of a rattlesnake’s bite.

He spoke then to the murder. Jackdaw was fidgeting while the brothers were calling out their words, but now he was still and silent. Likewise, General Fragit was motionless but attentive. When Ophrei spoke, it was with a voice not his own, and Nascus had the abrupt thought the old bird had been taken over by his father, or his father's father, so strong and authoritative was his tone. "You of the murder! Take heed. As it was when the crows gathered in Miscwa Tabik-kizi for the First Atonement, so it is for the Reckoning! This is the way of the order, and though none of you hold this memory beyond your own atonements, it is as deeply a part of you as your black feathers themselves! I will take these words to the wind, and the wind will tell them to my secret heart within." The rook closed his eyes then, with every bird watching and awaiting his command. "You will all follow the order of the rule, and the order will fall from me to the General and then to all the murder. This is not the time for feeble hearts weedy of burdens! I will tell the General his rule and the murder will follow as one! There will be one of these brothers to give from the heart, the heart to be shared among the many." The brothers all visibly shuddered at this. Sintus looked to his party, all of whom glanced expectantly back and forth from him to the rook.

"This is the spreading of the King's blood within the prince's veins to his murder. There will be another to offer his salt to the earth, so that the salt from the line of the King may go to enrich the soil of the field. These two will be sung of for years untold! Their sacrifice will be of equal gift for the strength of the field and the power of the murder. Their deaths will be only in body. The whole of the King will live on through the growing and the eating." He looked around the field. "And in the body of the newly crowned!" With that the field erupted in chaotic cawing, heavy black wings flogging the air. "This is the order!" Ophrei screamed above the ruckus.

"Now," spoke the rook, "the wind will tell the rule." And with that he closed his eyes again and began to shake. The murder became quiet, all eyes on the magician. To the sky he opened his eyes—their night's black was turned to a blood's red. His feathers seemed to take on a movement of their own, as if the wind were moving through them fiercely, but a gentle breeze was all there was. Then it became as if the wind itself were wrapping in a tiny tornado of gusts around the rook. The old bird stood firm but appeared to be fighting against the wind to keep from blowing away. The rest of the field was still, but the rook was within a storm. Then, as quickly as it had arisen, the wind about Ophrei ceased, leaving the bird tousled but still standing.

Then Ophrei turned to the brothers and leveled his still-red eyes at them. "Now, in the order I command, you are each to tell the tale of the Day of Creation, then tell the tale of your father's life."

"The Day of Creation?" Sintus laughed at this. "We all know the Day of Creation! What does this have to do with the Reckoning?"

"You will not question the Reckoning," answered the rook. "This is the way it has always been. Now I will distinguish the order in which you will tell. The wind has made it apparent to me."

Around the field the crows glanced to one another in confusion, but none spoke. Fragit kept his eyes steadily on the rook, attentive to every word. The old General moved a bit closer to Ophrei and out of the main circle. The rook turned his way and motioned for him to come near.

Fragit moved to the rook's side. "You will do precisely what the rook commands," said the General to the brothers. The look he gave them said, *I don't care that you are princes. You will follow the order.*

"Now, I announce the sequence," said Ophrei. "Milus will be first, followed by Sintus. The final will be Nascus."

"What?" Sintus was outraged. "I am the firstborn of the princes, and the rightful in line! What is this treachery?" He looked to his supporters, many of which made calls of agreement.

"You will do as commanded," said Fragit, stepping in close to the boastful bird. "You are under the rule of the Reckoning and will follow the order of the rook."

Sintus did not respond to this in voice but strutted around angrily, cawing in disgust. All eyes watched him. His court and allies responded loudly to his canting. The General and the rook only watched him warily. After a short tirade, the eldest brother glared at his sibling foremost in line. "Well, then, brother. Go on with it." Sintus turned to Ophrei. "What will he be giving? His salt or his heart, dear sage?"

The old rook did not respond, but directed his attention to the youngest. "Now, Milus, the hand of time is to you. Recount the Day of Creation. Then tell of your father's life."

Milus looked around the Murder's Field for support, but none was found. It appeared as if he was sure this was some trick, and someone was going to offer him the special word that would prove he was the rightful King. In truth, he was not worried about the need to be King . . . except that the one chosen would be the only one of the three to live.

He sniffled then called around the field, "I will now tell the story of Creation!"

The bird cleared his throat and shuffled his feet. "In the first night," he recited, "the Wind and the Earth were as one, but still each was alone. And during the dark the Earth slept, but the Wind never slept. And the Wind counted all it held within and also below and considered what could be made. And the Wind thought alone and gathered above the Earth and within that night pondered. Then, looking down upon the Earth and seeing the cold rock, the Wind thought to make a companion. And the Wind carried dust, and within the dust were feathers, but upon the Earth only the still black stone. And the dust from within the air settled upon the rock. This is so, as it was and as it is.

"And come morning the Earth woke and the stones sought to shake the dust from themselves and to create companions of their own, but alone the stones could not move, and the Wind seized them and lifted them up into itself. And within the Wind there was blood, as if red rain, and it took form, and the feathers settled around the stone and the blood gathered beneath the feathers, so the stones became bones and took form to fill the shape. And this meshing of bones, feathers, and blood became a living thing, and the Wind desired to keep the thing as its own. The Earth was greatly angry, for the Wind had taken from the Earth its stones. So the Wind held the thing it had created and called it Crow. This was all upon the first day. And the Earth and Wind have not ceased their battle since. And at night the Wind tears at the Earth, and come light, the Earth stares angrily up to the Wind. And Crow holds allegiance to the Wind, and curses the Earth and steals from it."

The field erupted in a chaos of shrieks and caws, the full murder in chorus, their tongues red and their eyes black. Edith, Milus's mother, looked around at her son's followers, smiling as best she could. "Eh, now that was quite well told," she jittered. "What say all you?"

To that she received a less than enthusiastic response. Still, she kept her smile.

The rook stared at the youngest brother, cold and certain, giving nothing away. The wind shuffled through his feathers. "Now, Prince. The tale of your father's life."

WITHIN THE BRAMBLE the three quail watched and listened. Ysil had heard the crow's tale of Creation before. Just as the quail learned the Quailsong, the crows likewise had their educations. He felt a bit confused, although some of this he had seen before when the crows took to field. The tale of Creation was told frequently, passed down from generation to generation, and he had hidden and listened to their tale more than once. The quail, like the crows, held an allegiance to the wind, but the quail heard the songs on the wind—and heard its laughter. He felt that most crows heard nothing but the rake of leaf upon branch and the whipping of grapevine. And though Ysil did not necessarily disbelieve the crow's tale of Creation, he certainly did not like the idea of a crow being the first creature. Why would the wind have created such an animal as crow before quail, or rabbit, or even hawk for that matter? Crows were annoying and loud.

Ysil knew the next part of the tale, when the wind made more crows to keep itself moving should it begin to die, in doing so ensuring it never would cease. He had heard the tale of how the earth made the mice and the rabbits next, for it was jealous of the wind and the crows only took from the earth and never gave back. He knew the tale of the first hawk, Gritnim, whom the wind created to take from the earth's creations, and how the crows had established the order. It was long down the line in the story when the quail were created. Only an afterthought for the wind, really; creatures of its own to gather over the earth and to live upon it. The wind sought to make them allies to the earth, yet obligated to the wind, doubly bound. There was little else about the quail in the crows' Creation story. Ysil was always let down that there wasn't more concerning his own kind. Crows were such a self-centered bunch, and arrogant.

But the bird did not carry on the Creation tale. Milus went into the tale of his father's life as commanded. This was something Ysil had never heard told, and he had a feeling something significant was about to occur, but what that might be, he had no idea.

MILUS WAS STAMMERING. He did not know what was expected of him, and he did not like the looks of the birds around him. They were all staring at him with expectation, and not a few of them were openly glaring at him with contempt. Even his few followers were looking at him questioningly and with suspicion.

"Come, brother," called Sintus. "It's a bit late in season for a locust to be caught in your throat!" There was a hesitant murmur of laughter through the murder.

Milus cleared his throat again, this time more of a frightened growl. "My father was born to be King! He was the son of a King as was his father before him." Milus was searching. "My father was the best King in the history of crows! He was raised by his father's second she-bird. His mother was born of royal blood, but was murdered in the great stone garden for the Atonement. It was a rook that took her life." He darted his eyes to Ophrei, who stared back, unmoving and without response or change. "She was offered as a curse to man for the good of all crows. My father spent his life as a good King—"

"Stop!" screamed the old rook without warning. "Silence," he said, and the youngest prince froze.

Then the old rook closed his eyes and began to shiver. He spoke first with a quiet tumble of words. Then, as he continued, his voice grew in intensity and volume.

"The day your father was born has been forgotten by your heart, bird. The day your father died lives stronger within your memory. You are of soundless gizzard, and in your passing your frailties will be totally consumed. Only your strengths will remain. In this you may celebrate."

Milus began to step back toward the outer ring. He glanced around in fear and desperation. His few supporters watched him uneasily. The rest of the murder began to caw softly and restlessly. The rook continued.

"The wind will consume and carry away what is given in dust. You are made of this: forged of dust and now a dispersion of it. You are the fodder for the worm, naught but a scattering of black feathers. You are the flavor for the murder! You will give from the heart!" This last Ophrei cawed in tremendous crescendo.

Milus hopped suddenly and in fearful tumble jumped to the sky, but Fragit was on him, dragging him down with greater weight.

"No!" screamed Edith. "No! Do not kill my son!"

But the rook's command had created a frenzy, and none heeded her pleas. Every crow took to wing and together formed a circle, its center over Milus and tightening like a whirlpool or tornado. With them came a great gust of wind from all four directions, driving the circling birds, Milus's band included. The whole of the winged group plummeted in upon the youngest brother, driving down fast and hard as a single great black beast. Even Edith, still bellowing her screams of defiance, was swept in with the rest. With the force of a terrible black storm, the full lot of them became one writhing mass of screaming, cawing fury.

To Ysil, watching in awe from the brush, it seemed as if each crow had gone insane at precisely the same time, controlled by a greater mind. No matter the cause of the insanity and bloodlust, and one for a child of the King at that, the reason for the naming was evident. Ysil would forevermore understand precisely why the great family of crows was known as a murder.

It was not long until the writhing mass of birds dissolved then formed back into the circle. On each and every beak were streaks of the prince's blood. Milus was gone, shredded. In his place was a distribution of black feathers and swaths of red across the freshly cut silage. Edith lay amid this gruesome scattering, her feathers soaked with the blood of her son. Then she began to thrash about, wailing in the greatest sadness ever known. The crows cawed loudly even after they moved away from the center and resumed form.

Ophrei stayed within the circle, a lone bird, specks of blood brightening his ebony feathers. The wind had expired, as still as if it had never blown.

When the birds quieted, Ophrei's gaze settled upon the eldest. "The time has come for your Reckoning, Sintus. You are to offer your version of the tales. You are to offer them to the wind, and the wind will be the judge."

Sintus shook in righteous anger, his own brother's blood dripping from his sharp beak. "Why should I not merely state the truth of my birthright? I should not be forced to honor this Reckoning. This is old and dying magic. The time for a new King has come, and most know I should be the one. Those who do not will soon be convinced." There was a nervous murmur of agreement from his devotees. Nascus remained calm. The General, inscrutable, eyed the eldest. The twelve sentinels watched Fragit for any sign of charge.

Ophrei chuckled a bit then quivered his feathers with a slight tremble. "You will abide by the Reckoning's order and carry on with the relation."

Then Sintus likewise laughed a bit and said, "Oh, all right, old bird! I'll play your needless game. Let me see . . . how does that old story go? Something like this, I think . . ." He began to hum a melody, something without ordered notes or tune, really a childlike da-da-ma-ma-dum with no sense to it. He broke into a dance as the melody continued. The old rook watched, his tremor stilling. Sintus's mindless humming continued. Then one of his followers, Darus by name, stepped into the circle and joined the dance.

"In the first night," he sang gaily, "the Wind and the Earth were making babes. And the Earth just lay there while the Wind had its way. And the Earth shook in earthquake and the Wind came in a hurricane! And looky what they made! Cold gray stones to mark the graves. Of course, the Wind was let down. Let me give you the best I can, my love! And it blew hard as it could and look what came out! Little black gods! Crows!" He continued the dance and song for a while, fearless and arrogant. Darus took his wing in beak and did a mock curtsy to the prince.

Ophrei watched, his expression unchanging. The rest of the murder was quiet with the exception of Sintus's group, who were forming into a company and whistling and cawing along with the eldest. Sintus broke out of the song and went back to the mindless humming and whistling with which he had begun. Darus moved back toward the outer circle but stayed closer to the prince than before the dance. Sintus did a final trot and ended his 'tale' with a jump and a short flight, spreading his wings to their fullest and calling out, "And that is the truth and I am here to tell it!" His group, which had assembled more distinctly since he began his song, exploded in laughter and support. For the most part, the rest of the murder was still and watchful, though a few did laugh nervously. Fragit did not move, nor did his guard.

Ophrei showed no sign of annoyance or amusement, just calmly said, "Now. Tell the story of your father's life."

Caught up in his fit, Sintus reacted as if he had just eaten a rotten apple. "The old King Crow was born to be a better King but never was! He slept most of his majestic life, though he bedded many fine black birds! Yes, that's it! Just slept, ate, and made babies! He has three sons official, but his bastards are many. Let me see—" He glanced around the field. "Why, there's one, two, seven, sixteen . . . Ah! Look at all my brothers and sisters unofficial! Not one of you would deny!" There was laughter throughout the field, some buoyant and some tense.

It was then that from his hiding place within the brush Ysil clearly saw Ophrei's feathers begin to rustle with a rise in the wind. He could not feel any breeze at all, and the murder seemed intent on Sintus's tale and did not notice. Abruptly the old rook began to quaver.

Cotur Ada put his wings around the younger quails and held them low. "Young ones. The kingship is about to be decided, surely. I have the feeling that Sintus's record is not to be approved."

To their left, within the brush at the bottom of a small hollow, there was a rustle and a panicky peep. Fear gripped Ysil. Was it a crow guard, searching for intruders? He froze and lifted his eyes to Cotur Ada, who was staring in the direction of the sound, his eyes wide.

"I do believe we have found our lost young ones."

Ysil stole another look and saw four eyes peeping out from beneath a blackberry bush. The eyes were those of Anur and Erdic, creeping through the bush to get a better view of the Reckoning. Now the two chicks stared right at Ysil, and with a look of shock in their eyes upon seeing the other quail, the chicks began to move to them. In great concern, Ysil noticed that the route they were about to take would bring the young ones within view of the field. Surely the crows were too busy to notice the two, but there was no way to know for sure. Ysil wanted to cry out in warning, but to do so would certainly alert the crows to their presence. He glanced up to Cotur Ada. The old quail's silence seemed to prove his fear; there was nothing they could do to halt the young ones' advance. Cotur Ada pressed his wings tightly over Monroth and Ysil, holding them down and keeping them still. Ysil heard a whimper and knew that on the other side of his grandfather's body, Monroth was crying in fright.

From the field Ysil heard the voice of Ophrei rising in rage. "You have shamed your father's memory and history! You were not born to be King; you were born to offer your salty blood to the field! You will succumb and lie down to have your breast opened!"

Silence spread throughout the murder, but for the wind, which had once again become a revolving gale. Small dust devils and frenzied gusts were enveloping the trees around, their leaves' undersides flashing brightly, twisting and bending in the storm's furor.

"I *am* the King!" called Sintus over the chaos of the wind. "I will offer nothing to this field but my rightful rule! I *will* be King of this field, though maybe not today! You are the one, old bird! It is you who will offer your blood to me! The field will just as hungrily drink yours as mine! You are not worthy of taking my blood."

Then Fragit rose up with the wind, his wings searing through the gusts with a horrible pounding. He began to bear down on Sintus, his guard of twelve just behind. It was like he had received some unspoken direction from Ophrei, who was struggling to stay afoot with the gale so strong. But before Fragit could get to Sintus, the whole of the eldest's followers intersected the General, beating their wings wildly and pecking him, and then the twelve were upon them all. The field filled with screams of pain and bloodlust as the two groups were consumed in mortal combat. While the chaos ensued, Sintus took to air, righteous fury driving his frenzied wings. He was quickly up to the sky and racing toward the tree line. As he flew he called out above the raging wind: "When I return, it will be at the lead of a great battalion of crows! And with coyotes and foxes under my command!"

And the wind bore down upon the fighters and watchers alike.

A small group of Sintus's league, Darus at lead, flew off after the prince. Ophrei screamed, "Fragit! The rogue is fleeing! You must away! You must pursue!" Fragit broke free from the foray and took after the rebels. The skirmishing continued, but some of the Guard flew off to assist Fragit. The fighting began to diminish as the prince's followers surrendered or died. The rest of the murder hopped around the field in rightful agitation.

Ophrei glared at Nascus, who was surrounded by the relative safety of his followers. The old rook flew over to the prince and, landing mere inches from him, lay down and spread his wings, his head turned under. This is for the crows the greatest sign of submission.

Jackdaw stood behind the rook, overcoming his shock. Following suit, he also lay down and tendered the same to the prince.

"Please, wise old bird, you need never bow to me," said Nascus.

The rook looked up but did not rise. "You are to be King. The wind has shown this to me. You will be King. It is my place to bow to you. You are chosen. But you will not wear the crown until your brother has poured his blood upon the field. It is an unwise thing he has done. It is not within the order. He must be captured and returned. And should the opportunity arise, it must be you to open his chest."

Nascus stared at Ophrei in seeming shock and misunderstanding. Then he raised his head, his face set in resolve.

"So be it," he said, and the wind abruptly ceased.

BANKA, WHO WAS the first under Fragit's command, struggled with one of the rebels. He pecked furiously at the rogue's head and stabbed his beak into an eye, and with a great jerk ripped it free from the skull. The injured crow jumped away and fell squawking to the field, its life pouring from the hole in its head, death soon falling upon it.

Heeding the General's command, Banka took to the air in pursuit of Fragit. As he neared the edge of the field, he saw two small brown shapes quivering within the brush. Quail. A new rage filled him. He bore down on the two small birds, the fury of battle still hot in his heart. *I'll stop and quickly deal with these before my commanded pursuit*, he thought. The birds, frozen in horror, helplessly watched his descent, the crow's awful eyes alight and his beak dripping red with blood.

COTUR ADA SAW Banka take to the air and fly directly toward the hidden chicks. Then he heard the crow caw loudly and turn downward in a redirected flight path toward the young ones. He had seen them! If Ada were to try to save the chicks, he would take the chance of exposing the two he sheltered beneath his wings now. All could die. If he did nothing, the two little birds would surely find death that afternoon. He briefly wrestled with the decision, but before he could move either way, an old and haggard form staggered out of the brush and stood between the descending crow and the babes.

"Stop, Banka! You fool among fools." It was Incanta, the elder. Her voice was shrill in righteous defiance. "You are the coward I have always known you to be, as was your father before! How dare you!"

But the angry crow did not slow down. He continued his dive. In seconds he would be upon the brave old bird and the frightened chicks just behind her.

Chapter Four

In the Vulture Field

SULARI, THE OLD gray hare, was nervous. He had set out with a certain number of animals in his care. There were five missing quail of late, and now Gomor the rabbit had disappeared. This was no good. Certainly by now Cotur Ada had found the two lost chicks and was on the way to join them at Olffey Field. But the group had been there for two moves of the sun, and it would soon be dark again. This would not do at all. Sulari had hoped for a swift return of the lost animals and their rescuers.

Ekbeth, the mother of the vultures, sat on a low branch of the great dead sycamore. The huge tree had been a lifeless skeleton for a long time but, strangely, had not withered or rotted. In fact, when Sulari had made his first journey to the vultures' field—a gesture of good faith, a trip he had made with his father when he was young—the tree had been dead then. The tree was pure white—all sycamores are white naturally, but this one was caked with the droppings of the fifty-some birds that called it home. All the vultures were the children of Ekbeth, or at least they called her their mother. Her nest was perched in the top of the tree.

The field itself, if it could really be called a field seeing as nothing grew within, was covered with bones. Bones of all types, from gnarled turkey bones to the bones of possums. From the bones of coyotes to the bones of the vultures themselves. Some of these animals had died here by their own choosing, but most of the bones were flown here after being picked clean. Sulari's father had told him these were remembrances to the vultures—almost prayers. But to the hare, they seemed more like trophies.

Sulari recalled that first trip to the field very clearly. He remembered how he had been dreadfully afraid, asking his father why they had to go. How his father had said that the vultures carried the spirits of all animals who died to the Great Field, that in life we pay our respects at least once (this being the way of the hare), for in death, we are, at least in part, eternally theirs. Father said this was a good thing. He said that we were, birds and animals alike, all bound to return to the earth; but a small part would go to the sky . . . the part that belonged to the vultures.

Ekbeth watched on high from her roost as the hare and his company approached the great dead tree. She offered her hideous, gaping scowl to give cheerful greeting, and for the mother of all vultures, this was the best she could do.

"You are welcome here, Sulari of man's field," she said. "You are welcome here in life as you are in death."

"Thank you, Mother," said Sulari. "We have come under command of the murder. The King is dead and the Reckoning for the new King has come."

"Yes, I have heard." She gazed to the far side of the sycamore where three mourning doves sat, perched precariously on an outer limb. "We have sent envoys. They will be there come evening."

Doves flew skyward, though quail did not. And though Sulari thought he had seen these doves before, he was certain they were not of his field. Doves traveled as the seasons commanded, and these lines never changed. One dove who moved through this area in the fall would likely not move through the Murder's Field, or the man's field as the vulture called it (the vultures gave no credit to the crow's claim), unless they both lay on the same migration route. Perhaps it was through these lines that the rumor of doves traveled? Perhaps whisperings on the wind? Perhaps this is how they had come to know of the death of the King? Sulari never considered doves too long, and he pushed off these thoughts of the little birds.

Cotur Mono and Rompus moved up next to Sulari, for comfort's sake and to gather in the talk with the vulture. "The new King will be crowned tonight," said Ekbeth. "Unless one offers disregard. But that has happened only once that I know of, and long before my time." Ekbeth seemed to forget what she was talking about for a moment and stared at the sky. Then she examined Sulari. "You are too young to remember the last Reckoning, eh, hare?"

"Aye, Mother. It was before I was birthed, even. Was early in the winter of my father's time. He did not speak much of it, only to say that he was excited to see the new young King. Did the animals come to this field with the Reckoning before?"

"Yes, yes they did, and they always have. Thinking of it now, your father was here, as was your mother. Of course they are here now." Sulari gazed out upon the blanket of white bones covering the ground and fidgeted. "Now, each time the animals come to shelter here we ask the same question, and we will ask it of you now." With that some of the vultures flew down and perched upon the branch with Ekbeth. Harlequin moved up into the forward group, closer to Cotur Mono. Ekbeth glanced at the young beautiful bird, and for a moment Sulari thought he saw something dark gather in the old vulture's eye. Was it hunger?

Then she spoke, the vultures around her joined, whispering the same words in time through their haggard and stained beaks. As the chorus of voices sang the offer, Sulari chilled. It was a song, and though the words held rhythm, the melody was vague and sad, as if sung by a toad trapped beneath the sod during winter's freeze.

Come, furry and feathered
Come, strong; and come, weak
Come; gather your forms
Near our guarding beaks.

As you live we will keep you
Protect from on high
And tend you and feed you
'Til you happily die.

And then we will bear you
Up to the clouds
Tight in our bellies
Our bodies your shrouds.

And offer your spirit
To the Great Field
Just rest with us now
'Til to death you shall yield.

The animals below stared up in dead silence. The mice were still (which was rare) and watched with anxious intent. The quail and rabbits were all huddled together in tight groups, their wide eyes turned up to the vultures and the great white tree in taut dread. Only the golden rat seemed uninterested. He sat gnawing on a gristly raccoon bone he had found. For the longest moment, there was only silent brooding, the animals entranced. It was that those on the ground were too shocked to respond and those on the tree too eager to ask again. The vultures likewise stared down at them, their mouths agape and their eyes keen.

Finally, Ekbeth spoke, this time alone. "I would offer you this as I did to your father and his before. They turned us down. You could be a King of your own right here, Sulari . . . a King for a while. Will you be so wise and brave as to take this offer?" She inspected the visitors, her big bald head jerking from one to another of them in a jagged rhythm. "Will any of you?"

The whole of the animals quivered and, as one, took a single step back.

His nose cold and beginning to run, Sulari turned to Cotur Mono, who in turn looked to Rompus. Rompus, who was just getting over his flogging from the day before, shook his head. He would not speak out this time, though surely they were safe from any attack from the vultures.

"Um, thank you, O great and wise Mother, for your offer," responded the hare timidly. "We are here as a whole and must surely return to our home as that same whole when we can. We are blessed by your most gracious offer, but we truly miss our home. We must return to it. Surely you will not be offended by our leaving—"

"Oh, we do understand. None we have asked have joined us immediately. Some do come in time." The bird motioned a black wing to a corner of the field where a huge old deer lay dazed and still. Sulari had not noticed the animal before. It could not be denied that the deer was very much alive. It scrutinized them, its antlers swaying as it turned in their direction. The deer was fat, and the hare thought it would not move if it could. Then Sulari caught movement just beside the deer and saw, with some shock, a grayed coyote basking lazily only a few feet from the antlered buck. The coyote was gnawing on the bone of some unidentified animal, and though the deer was easily within a jump's distance, neither animal seemed interested in the least at the other's presence. Sulari now understood. Some animals came here when they could no longer gather food or fend for themselves. They came here to let the vultures care for and feed them until they died. Care for them in exchange for . . . what?

"Oh, great Mother!" called Sulari. "We will keep your offer in our hearts, all of us, I am sure, but for now we beg you to allow our group temporary refuge here within the safety of your field."

The old bird of carrion gapped her beak in her peculiar way of smiling. "Yes, you may stay. And you may leave at your own will. And whenever you do return, in whatever capacity that may be, you will be greeted with fervent stomach."

"Thank you, O wise Mother," said Sulari as he considered Rompus. The badger was quivering ever so slightly. His old friend looked back at him, trying to smile.

Chapter Five

The Grandfather's Command

BANKA BORE DOWN upon the old quail staring up at him in defiance. At the last moment before he crashed into Incanta, the crow seized up his wings and came to a furious stop. Planting his feet inches from the quail, the bigger bird pounded his wings.

"You are forbidden here in this time!" cried Banka. "For this you must die, bird! You are not allowed!"

Incanta rose to her tallest and glared into the eyes of the bloody crow. "You are a coward and a murderer, Banka, a bastard and a child of none! As I die within your beak, so will my bravery live on. As you kill these babes, so will your cowardice be forever consummated! You will kill us with no good gain." She did not waver to either side at all, only glared up at the crow in insolence.

It was then that Anur hopped and awkwardly tried to make flight. He took off clumsily and was loud in his desperate departure. Banka took after him and in mere seconds had the small bird on the ground.

"No!" cried Incanta.

The chick cried out in fear and pain as the crow drove its claws into its soft, feathered flesh. Banka, perched above his catch, only glowered at the elder bird.

"Do not hurt the little one!" she cried.

Incanta, who could not fly at all, ran over to Banka with all the speed she could muster. She had momentarily forgotten Erdic, who, though he surely could have flown to safety in the bedlam, lay still as death upon a blanket of freshly fallen leaves.

Incanta attacked Banka with what fury she could muster, jumping at him, pecking and screeching. From within the brush, not far away, Ysil could hear the crow begin to laugh.

It was then that Cotur Ada made his decision. He turned to the younger quail.

"You must flee, young ones," he said firmly. "You must away to beyond the river. I must try what I can to save the babes and the elder."

Ysil was confused and scared. "Beyond the river? What do you mean, Grandfather?"

"You must carry a plea to the hawk Pitrin. Take the path of which I told you. Speak my name to him. I pray it saves you from his claws. Tell him his father begs him return to the field to bring order." Ysil's confusion grew. *Father?* "I fear a great war is upon us, children. I feel there are far darker things at work here than just a rascal prince, a thing far more dangerous. You must convince him not to harm you. Bring with you this." And with that Cotur turned back his head and pulled out a long tail feather with his beak, then laid it down before Ysil.

"Beg him come, Ysil, Monroth. Ysil, you must carry the feather. Tuck it within your breast to keep it safe. Be vigilantly watchful after you cross the river. He could take you easily, and I pray he does not before he sees the feather. This token will be your only safeguard. You must trust me when I tell you he will not harm you when you show him my feather. I regret it is to the two of you that I must pass this order, but, alas, fate has handed this to you. Hear your command. You must follow." With that Cotur Ada slowly and carefully moved away from the two.

"Of course, I can handle anything, Cotur Ada," said Monroth with a burst of sudden pride, "but you speak nonsense. You are no father to any hawk." Ysil felt Monroth's former statement to be only more boasting, but he kept this to himself. Monroth's latter statement he was in agreement with. He knew his cousin bird was as frightened by the notion of actually seeking out a hawk as he was, maybe even more so. What could Cotur Ada mean saying such a thing: a quail the father of a hawk?

"There is no time for your questions. Follow my order." Then he rustled even farther away. He looked back only once more. "Be still, my children. Be still until the dark has fallen. You may find friends in unexpected places and with unexpected faces . . . so take care whom you trust . . . and whom you do not!" And Cotur Ada, the eldest of the quail, took to the air and straight toward the laughter of Banka and the screaming of Incanta and the chick.

WHEN HE HAD been very young Cotur Ada had gotten into a fight with a certain young crow. He had been at the field's edge with his father, Vanda, and his brothers eating the grain of the season's harvest. The man had raked the field two days previous, and the moon was waning toward dark. The animals had already stored away, but the field still held great bounty. Ada knew that this was the time of best gathering, and his father made sure the chicks did not miss a bite that was available. The winter months were hard, and they needed to fatten up in preparation. Young Ada was contentedly busy with his eating. He did not notice that around him all had grown quiet, nor did he see the reason for their silence. It was Banka's presence that had silenced the group.

Ada was bashed upon the head and knocked to the ground. He tumbled in pain. "You are all to leave the field now!" commanded Banka. When he had approached, Ada's father evidently had been too far away to notice the intrusion of the crow. The rest had watched in fearful silence as the much larger crow had approached the unknowing Ada.

"Why did you do that?" Ada had cried.

"You quail are always sneaky!" young Banka had called. "You think this field is yours, but you're wrong! This is the crows' field! And we answer to no one!"

"Ada is my son," Cotur Vanda had said, moving in swiftly beside the wounded chick. "He is too young for your thrashing. Take this up with me instead." The brave quail had stepped straight up and faced Banka, their beaks nearly touching.

Sadly, Banka *had* taken it up with Vanda. He flogged Ada's father with his wings and screamed malicious caws until the blood turned Vanda's gray feathers to a dusty red.

Looking back through the seasons, Cotur Ada knew that his father had never really recovered from that beating.

The young and angry crow had broken two of Vanda's toes and they had healed badly. One day Vanda had been gathering blueberries with two of Ada's brothers. An old and desperately hungry fox had attacked. Vanda had flushed up with the younger quail but had taken off badly. The fox took him down, its eyes gone a dull gray with age and the lust for blood. Cotur Ada always wondered if his father had been just a little slower because of his broken toes.

He was careful not to fly too high, hoping not to be seen by the other crows, whose desperate fray was only beginning to abate. He had an idea, and though it was a dire measure, certainly for him and perhaps for all, he felt it the only chance to save the chicks. It was a measure that would work only if Banka proved to be the fool he thought him to be. He flew in and landed close to Banka and the quail, who were locked in a sort of one-sided tussle, with the large crow holding down the chick while the elder tried her best to get him off. "Stand down, Grandmother!" Cotur Ada cried when he landed.

Banka stared back in surprise, as did Incanta. She fell back from the crow, exhausted and bleeding from the beak, the injury likely from her own efforts. There was no sign the crow had attacked her, nor for that matter was there a mark on his black body either.

"Ah!" roared Banka. "So there are to be four to die! How many more quail are hidden in the brush? This is an insult from quail to the order of crows! Your blood will be shared by many today!"

"You have found a treasure here, O wise crow," said Cotur Ada, "and you don't even know it yet. Our placement here may be an offense to the crows, but on consideration you may find a benefit. You may suffer a boon for your own rite. You have the mother of many and the grandmother of innumerable at your hand. And I will speak for her. She will make you an offer." Incanta glared at Cotur Ada. Uncertainty was upon her face, but she said nothing. She lay prone, the rage still dancing in her eyes.

"What nonsense is this you are speaking, little bird?" Banka questioned.

"Ah, it is not nonsense in the least. You must know that to a quail the life of the chick is much more valuable than the life of the egg—the delicious egg." Cotur Ada said this last thing with a raised emphasis. "Between myself and the grandmother here, we know the whereabouts of at least two dozen hidden nests. These are secrets kept from the mink, the muskrats, the rats, and, of course, the crows."

A light of interest appeared in Banka's eye. "What would you offer that I may not demand?" he said, blood beginning to dry on his beak.

Cotur Ada looked to Incanta for some support. She granted none but kept her silence.

"What I offer you is a season's eggs in exchange for the lives of these chicks and the elder. Not only that, but I offer you my blood also."

Banka's eyes grew wide, a new hunger mingling with bloodlust. "Yes," he said. "Yes, I do believe we can make this trade."

From their hiding place in the brush, Ysil and Monroth heard these words. They heard, and the vast fear that had been clouding their breath consumed them even more.

They listened as Cotur Ada told Banka where to find the eggs, the hidden precious nests. But his words were vague, and Banka, so sure of himself, did not question. Ysil wondered if the crow could find the nests even if Cotur Ada told him the exact location. And so it was that Banka did prove his ignorance, for this time of year, there were no eggs in the nests at all.

The cawing sounds of battle continued to dissipate. Then, from far away, he heard the cawing crows on approach. Ysil knew that voice. The General was returning.

HIGH ABOVE THE field, a vee of geese soared. The leader had flown this particular route all his life and was nearing his turn to move back to the rear of the vee. He knew it would be dark before his turn would come again at lead, and surely he would also begin the next morning behind. He was looking for a place to land and take rest and find food before his turn was past, as he knew that the next in line was young and might choose a lesser option. Geese do not follow any but the leader, and, likewise, the leader of any vee would change many times during the day. None behind ever questioned the leader. He knew they were nearing a field where a murder of crows resided and many animals about it. He also knew that the man who farmed the field would have likely reaped by now and that there should be grain for the taking. He saw the field below and began to descend.

As it came closer into sight, the bird gasped and honked. Scattered about the field were many dead forms of sizable black birds. There had been a great battle here. He counted some nine dead and a good few writhing in pain. The geese flew low enough to smell the blood of battle, so even though they also smelled fresh grain, they veered away from the field and took off in pursuit of the heights. And as they flew upward, a small dove flew to the leader of the flock and came close to his ear. The dove whispered of much that had befallen the field and those who dwelled within it. Then the dove banked away, staying high above the chaos below.

The leader goose decided that resting in this particular area was ill-thought. They would fly as far away to the south as they could while the time in lead was his.

The geese soared higher, passing the news from one to another. Three dark birds passed far beneath, flying just above the treetops.

FRAGIT LANDED IN the field at a high speed, barely slowing when he touched ground and continuing his run straight to the side of Nascus and Ophrei. Fragit's third in command, a huge bird with dark and vicious eyes and a long cut across his chest, landed as Fragit did and approached the bequeathed and the rook. Fragit was covered in blood from tip of beak to filthy feet.

"Many of the traitors turned and faced our attack when we were scarce out of earshot. If not for the strength of my band, I surely would have been overtaken." Much of the blood on Fragit was from the traitor crows, but not all. "Some six of the traitors are yet to be accounted for, as I see four dead on this field. We killed four within the forest, but oh, ours is the greater loss! Five of my guard lay dead within the woods and five dead here. Only the three of us remain. But shame! Banka is not accounted for at all! I was hoping to see him here." He turned to Nascus. "Prince, these are dire times. You and your own must now join ranks with us." The prince nodded. "Some of us must guard the field and, first, you, my prince, while I must away with a number to seek your turncoat brother."

Fragit stood tall and scanned the field. "Order to all! Order to all! Reform circle!"

It took a few minutes as the wounded rose and spread out, but when all those able to stand were back in circle, it was clear the impact of the treacherous revolt. All counted, there were ten of the guard dead, two crows from the general army and eight traitors. Twenty from a murder of fifty-nine. With the six conspirators escaped, only thirty crows gathered in a vague circle.

"Traitorous quail!" called Ophrei, pointing to the woods. "All this blood, and still we are forced to spill more!"

All eyes turned to follow the rook's gaze. Staggering out of the brush was Cotur Ada, the eldest of the quail, with Banka of the guard close behind. He walked purposefully and upright toward Ophrei, a clear conviction branded in his eyes. He showed not an ounce of fear.

Chapter Six

Watchers and Eavesdroppers

YSIL FOLLOWED HIS grandfather's command to remain still, more out of fear and self-preservation than for the sake of respect. He watched while Cotur Ada made his offer to the crow Banka and heard with dread. He knew that even if the crow were to take the offer from his grandfather, it would surely mean the death of the elder quail. When Banka had agreed, Cotur Ada urged the babes to go with the elder Incanta and never look back. Through all this, Incanta did not speak one word. Only upon departure did she look back to Cotur Ada.

Before disappearing down a quail's trail hidden beneath a trestle of cloaked panic-grass and bull thistle, with a voice feeble but definite, she spoke: "You may very well command thc car of the King-in-waiting with your last words, likewise the sorcerer and also the General. What will you do with your tongue, old bird?" With that she ushered the chicks into the brush and disappeared. She was nearly blind, but she knew the trail by heart. Ysil said a prayer she would find her way, for the day was wearing on and the dark would soon come. He prayed them safe haven through the night.

Monroth and Ysil lay as still as possible, watching and trying to hear what Cotur Ada and Banka were saying, but they could make out none of it, for now they spoke in hushed tones. Then the crow pressed the quail through the brush at the edge of the field and then into it. Ysil and Monroth watched helplessly as Cotur Ada walked to the murder and to his fate. Behind him walked Banka, needing to do little to urge him on.

Gomor was bored. The day in the Vulture Field was hot and the wind was still. And besides that, it was creepy and strange here. He much preferred his home den. Adventure was exciting and all, but home was home and that was that. He wished he had been asked to go with Ysil and Monroth. He considered them upon a true quest, albeit dangerous.

He decided to go over and get a better look at the deer and coyote resting on the far side of the field. After some coaxing, Cormo had gone with him and, more easily, Harlequin. It was of no worry to be near the deer, but the coyote was different.

"It must be safe if the deer is just lying there unconcerned with the closeness of the predator," said Harlequin.

So, taking to a tight group, and edging inch by inch closer to the coyote, their eyes locked on his, the three came within speaking distance of the adopted residents. Both animals considered them, flicking the ever-present early fall flies with their tails, the deer chewing the cud and the coyote a bone.

Neither animal granted the arrival of two young quail and a rabbit much notice. It was Cormo who spoke first.

"Hello," he said. The deer just glared back.

"Hello, my tasty one." It was the coyote who answered.

Gomor shivered. "Um, hello, sharp tooth. Uh, what brings you both to the Vulture Field?"

The coyote was exceedingly old, and it seemed an effort for him to offer a reluctant answer: "I suppose it could be said that it is the daily guarantee of a bountiful feast that brought us here. . . and keeps us. However, I must admit that tomorrow holds nothing. Eh, Sephel? Easy here for us today, but tomorrow is meaningless. What say, old friend?"

The deer moaned and shifted. "I would admit there is much truth to what you say, Cago, much truth. But I say tomorrow be damned. Ones as old as we cannot claim much of a tomorrow bearing these withered forms. At least here we can be friends, you and I. I worry not for your teeth, and you lust not for my flesh. Free at last from the bonds that have held us for so long."

The coyote laughed. "Little ones, come rest with us for a while. All you must do to be cared for is to lie down. No announcements needed. The vultures will bring you food."

"We don't need the vultures to care for us; we are only here passing through," said Harlequin. "We have a home."

"Oh, pretty one," said Sephel, "from here, you will certainly be upon a circular journey. Your path will lead you back to this place one day, by your own will or not." And with this the coyote and deer both laughed darkly, then fell into an easy silence, returning to their chewing.

The quail and rabbit alike shivered. Then Cormo said to Gomor, "Let's leave these two alone. They are past insane." Neither Gomor nor Harlequin argued.

The three went back to the main group of animals for a while as the vultures had brought in hay from the fields near and also branches covered with late berries. Some of the berries had soured. Only the elders were allowed these, and they brought much happiness to the mind and body. Too many of these soured berries and the eater would become dizzy and mindless. The young were not privy. Harlequin sat down to eat beside Cotur Mono. The leader of the quail had consumed a few of the sour berries, but not too many. He was sentimental. They talked of the day and of the dealings with the vultures. They spoke lightly for a bit, then Cotur Mono narrowed his eyes upon the younger.

"So, my little one, which of your suitors has caught your eye?" he asked her.

"Oh, Grandfather, I can admit to none!" she said. "All are but chicks, and I love only one. You know that! Only you." She toyed with him.

He smiled back. "My love, you are the joy of my life, just as your grandmother was before you. Your grandmother. I do miss her."

Sadness overtook the younger quail. "I miss her also. From early waking light until darkness of sleep I think of her. And with the closing of dusk I dream of her."

Cotur Mono sighed. "Of all my children—let me tell you a secret—of all my children, you are my dearest. I see so much of her in your heart." He saw that Harlequin was crying.

Harlequin's eyes twinkled with the love she felt for the strong, wise bird. "Grandfather," she said, "there is one whom I have caught within my heart, and I do feel I am within his."

"Oh, your whispering heart! I believe I do know of whom you speak, my pretty. You speak of your old friend? The grand chick of Cotur Ada? By name, Ysil?"

She laughed. "Oh, Grandfather, why do you jest with me? He is too much a friend to be within the space of my heart! You only pretend not to know. I speak of Monroth!"

The old quail's feathers quivered a bit, as if a breeze had arisen, but there was no wind. He stared at her for a passing instant then went on. "Oh, yes, surely he is strong and full of wit. Fine young bird, yes, fine." He coughed, and for a moment, Harlequin thought her grandfather had breathed in a moth.

Gomor and Cormo were eavesdropping behind them, close enough to hear her speaking, and when she mentioned Monroth they looked at each other in amazement. So she did hold a place within her heart for Monroth! This was a bit of a shock, but most of all Gomor considered this to be a sad thing. For even though Ysil had never said it aloud, the rabbit knew his friend held her within his heart. The two then moved a bit away where they could speak freely.

"Monroth! What a shame," said Cormo. "Monroth bears more cowardice beneath his wings than Ysil will ever leave with his droppings."

"You speak the truth, bird," said Gomor. "Were I a quail, I would likewise be holding a place within for her." He looked around to see for sure the others were too far to hear. "Let us go away now. On the journey here I sighted a hollow log, empty and huge. We could make it there by nightfall and spend the dark hours within. Then, come morning, we could hurry home. Far ahead of the rest we would be. What do you say, bird?"

It did not take Cormo long to consider. "Yes. Let's do this," he answered.

And with this last word the two stole away. And none saw them leave except Harlequin, who had noticed them conferring and looked after her friends.

COTUR ADA WALKED with the stride of one who knows his fate and, though saddened by it, is nonetheless fearless to face what is to come. Ophrei watched his approach with trepidation.

"You are a fool, Cotur Ada," said the rook. "You are a fool to be in this field today."

"He watched the whole of the Reckoning," said Banka. "He admitted this to me and certainly will to you likewise."

The old quail walked up to Ophrei and, shaking his feathered bonnet with gathered resolve, stared directly into the listener's eye. The General stood very close, watching the rook for any sign.

"Though the certainty seems evident, I must ask: Is what Banka says true?" asked Fragit.

"Wisdom is in deed, not tongue," answered Cotur Ada.

"Why are you here?" asked Ophrei. "Why have you come to be a witness of this most sacred rite? To what purpose do you defy the decree, old bird? You know the cost of such insurrection, yes? This deed of yours is not of wisdom but of folly."

"My deed is clearly understood by some, and most surely not seen by you, rook, not for now. But there may come a time," said Cotur Ada. "I have chosen as my life's last endeavor this intrusion. That with my sacrifice, perhaps your hearts will hear. Now, before you make your judgment on me and pronounce my fate, I ask that you, General, and you, Ophrei"—he looked around the murder, every bird scowling and quiet—"and all of you! I beg you, hear my warning plea!"

"We will hear no plea for mercy, quail," said Fragit. "We are crows. We offer no mercy when the order has been broken. Your fate is already chosen."

"I seek no reprieve, General. What I ask is only for your ear, and I ask that you listen with your hearts, all of you. That is, if you have the heart to open."

Ophrei quaked in anger. "What is your plea, then, Cotur Ada, you who are numbered with the damned?"

"I beg of you to send an envoy over the river. To the place where Pitrin the hawk keeps his home. Beg of him to return." He looked around the field. "Who of you remembers when the wolves were here? Not I. I have heard the tales. Rook? You remember?"

"Aye, I do. Was a dire time," said Ophrei. Then he laughed, darkly. "Of what consequence is that? And why would any desire a hawk to return here?"

"I had come to believe that the strength of King Crow Mellori and the order he commanded held a balance here." Cotur Ada turned to General Fragit. "General, what was the claim Sintus made as he fled? Did he not claim to make his return with a battalion of coyotes and foxes? I fear it will not be only coyotes and foxes with which he returns."

The murder began a murmur.

"Of what nonsense do you speak?" asked Ophrei.

"I beg of you, send an envoy over the river. Beg Pitrin to return. Tell him"—and with this Cotur Ada trembled visibly—"tell him his father sent you."

"His father." Fragit laughed. "And who might that be?"

Cotur Ada, the eldest of the quail, lowered his head. "It is I," he said.

HIDDEN AWAY, YSIL and Monroth took in the words of the old quail. What could his grandfather mean: *the father of a hawk*? Out in the field Cotur Ada stood, his head lowered. The crows around him were laughing and murmuring at his ridiculous words. Ysil gaped in wonder at the feather his grandfather had given him. He must be planning some trick. But what? Ysil thought it a vastly dangerous thing his grandfather was doing, and though he struggled to find such, he could grasp no understanding of it.

Below, Cotur Ada, the eldest of the quail, began a song. With the first note, every crow froze silent. His voice was childlike and sweet at times, at times dark and full of warning. And as his melody rose, it settled the wind, and all listened intently, those upon the field and the watchers from their hiding place.

The Invocation of Cotur Ada

Long sung since time has passed
This song of golden field,
And here I've spent my weary life
To pick through meager yield.

Lupus Rex

I am known as Cotur Ada,
The eldest of the quail,
Now lend your ear and hear my plea
And hearken to my tale.

Do you recall past hungry days?
The dreadful worried nights?
When fearful quail would rise up meek,
To seek come morning light?

Every rabbit nibbled cautious,
And badger horded food.
Though mole he worried not a lot
For sleeping buried brood.

And jay gave early warning quick
A twitch of wing then gone.
And golden finch kept to her nest
With warning sounding song.

But we were hardly sheltered safe
By hiding in the brush,
When out we sneaked come morning light
None would watch o'er us.

That pale winter she daily came
And with no protection.
Starvation pushed us from our nests;
She took her selection.

She fell upon our number's kind
And on my loved ones dined,
The slower and the older ones,
The younger left behind.

But we were choiceless in those days,
For we must seek the grain,
Winter holds no greater bounty
Save what we store away.

She nested high up in the fir
And that year tended young;
We damned their cursed sharpened beaks,
With feasting bloody tongues.

High on his roost sat old King Crow
In council with the wind,
Sleepy and fat on robins' eggs,
Stinking of shed snakeskin.

We gathered up all true and brave
And told the King our fear.
He frowned and preened his dirty wing,
His murder roosting near.

Incanta spoke not one lone word
But wept before his feet:
Her dear babe chick taken away
By hawk's strong spiked beak.

Lupus Rex

A worn and angry old grey squirrel
Petitioned to the King:
But as he spoke the murder laughed,
Their cawing deafening.

"You're wise and brave, Your Majesty,
Please make this hawk to leave!"
But old King Crow fell fast asleep
And did not hear our pleas.

And eager Nijra went ahead
As younger quail will go,
And down upon him came the hawk,
Her talons clasping low.

She lifted him up to the sky
And brought him to her nest.
She fed her screeching babies' mouths
Upon bird's opened chest.

So back we trudged with heads hung low,
Our spirits sunk in hate,
For now our numbers were but few
(So many dead of late),

Back to our brambly hidden home,
Where sad all night we cried
And prayed that with the coming morn'
The hawk be satisfied.

And early I did rise to seek,
As seeking's what we do,
The little grain and winter's feed
To carry the day through.

With fearful heart I crept to field
'Neath hungered, desperate skies
And hoped to find a spot of green
And not death from on high.

And there beneath the sleepy sun
Just near a mouse's lair
A feathered form fought to set free
Its wing from man's sharp snare.

And in amazement I drew close
To see who was entwined.
In shock I found the murd'rous hawk
Entangled in the line.

I drew in close to see if she
Were too bound to break free.
She turned up quick with dying gasp
And set her eyes on me.

Red blood was flowing from her wing,
A gash deep in her side.
Her fury spent, she lay there, weak,
So bound up, neatly tied.

I looked to her and said, "Well now,
You've met untimely end.
Your bones we'll scatter 'cross this field,
Your feathers to the wind."

She stared at me and from her mouth
There came a saddened cry.
She said, "I ask you hearken to
My begging 'fore I die.

"I implore you heed my memory,
Barely out of my nest,
When quail in number were but few
With hawks' and wolves' contest.

"We had no food for weeks on end—
My brothers, sisters dead—
Wolves gorged fat on the dwindled quail
And ravaged rabbit's bed.

"And when the squirrel and dove were gone
And on wild feeding stopped,
The wolves grew brave and preyed upon
The lazy pasture stock.

"And man was pricked by this offense
To find his cattle slain,
And shot and killed the wolves until
There was but one remained . . .

"A young gray wolf, so fast and proud,
Into the forest ran
And once again a prayerful calm
Settled on the land.

"These times I'd say none can recall,
'Cept turtle—mute and still—
When man our common enemy
Did all the strong wolves kill.

"And if you were to let me die
And rot into the ground
Who then would feed my babies' mouths
With mother not around?

"But set aside my final beg,
And take great warning: Heed!
I only take so many now
Because I've mouths to feed . . .

"And beak and talon are but trite
When held to claw and teeth,
Should I pass on there may return
The wolf to gain this keep.

"Fly, I beg you, bless my babes
And feed their bellies good.
It won't be long they'll learn to fly
Their purpose understood."

"And whom to them will we then feed?
Our young, our old, our weak?
Shall I tear my child's precious flesh?
And push it to their beaks?"

Weak she gasped a slow reply:
"Feed worms or grubs or flies.
It won't be long they'll need your care,
Their nature realized."

And as she talked all gathered round,
Our figures small and frail.
The dove, a badger, mole, and rat,
The rabbits, mice, and quail.

Still we watched in silence deep
As, witness to her weeping,
We viewed her tortured suffering,
'Til death did claim it's keeping.

We left her there and went our way
And danced until the night
And through the dark, we shut our ears
To starving babies' cries.

The next night the cacophony
Of weeping was still there,
But not as loud, as surely some
Had died without her care.

The foll'wing day but one still wailed
From there within the nest
I pressed my wings tight to my ears,
Prayed, "Babe, give up contest!"

But then the next night still it cried
And I had made my will
To fly up there, and in the nest,
The screaming infant kill.

But when I looked upon its form
So frail and near-death weak,
I scraped the bark and found a grub
And pushed it to its beak.

The little bird snapped up the worm;
Hungrily gulped it down.
And once it ate, it closed its eyes
And sleeping made no sound.

But come the evening following,
The little one cried need.
As day set off in losing light,
The poor thing I did feed.

None knew that I fed him each night
And learned to love the thing
The hawk took me as father
My tending, pampering.

And large it grew and hungered more
And gained in needful size,
But though I brought it many bugs
Its need did not subside.

Then one cold morning, early still,
I heard the rustling brush,
And out I peeked with fear to find
Just what the trouble was.

And there, with rabbit's dead form clutched
In talons sharp and strong,
My foster son stood all aglow,
As if he'd done no wrong.

With purpose filled he looked at me,
Said, "Father, now I see
I'm not meant to subsist on grubs,
'Tis fresh meat that I need!"

"No!" I screamed. "You murderer!
You fiend, you've killed my kind!"
There came a pained and bloody tear
Formed crimson in his eye.

I knew beyond a bitter doubt
What I had done for love
Was only for a greater sin
Than what good done thereof.

The old King Crow flew laz'ly down
And landed at my wing
His feathers worn and specked with white,
His grimace frightening.

He watched on, frowning thoughtfully
As I spoke to my son,
"You must go now! Never return.
Your time to leave has come!"

The hawk, he made the saddest sound
That I have ever heard.
The mournful wretch flew swift away,
The screeching, broken bird.

And as I watched, he disappeared
Into the morning sky,
And broken, whispered soft to him
A father's sad good-bye.

King Crow he stepped then chuckled smart.
"Your child is grown, I see.
I am much vexed that he has gone.
His presence we did need."

Then crow he flew up to his perch
And closed his eyes to sleep,
And I cried over rabbit's form
For I had loved him deep.

And now we are so many here
And so few killed as prey,
We are fearless through the night,
And careless through the day.

But lately when the moon's been full
I preen and do not sleep
And listen for the howling wolf
The hawk had promised me.

When Cotur Ada finished the song, the field remained stonily quiet. The rook marveled at the quail. "The father of the hawk, eh? If what you say is true," canted Ophrei in calm, "he *will* still recognize you as his father. Alas, Elera lied about there being a surviving wolf, surely a ploy to trick your mercy, akin to the same ploy you attempt today, eh? There is not a bit of truth to it. But I find myself believing your tale in some part. Quail were always a soft lot. Your sympathy for the hawk chick brought the death of your friend. Sympathy can be such a sticky thing. Clasped you to fate, it did. All dealings with hawks bring death, for your kind and, at times, for crow kind. We need not seek Pitrin and beg his return. For this field, the order of the hawk is past. The order of the crow is in its place. No wolf will come. This is nonsense. Perhaps we will seek a council with the turkeys and offer them a portion of the next harvest for their alliance, or even with the deer if we must. With their help, we need not worry about the few foxes Sintus may convince to allegiance. Surely not the first snake or bobcat will join him. And as far as wolverines—there are no more wolverines, as there are no more wolves. And if Sintus would seek to ally his cause with the father coyote, the beast will eat him straight away."

Cotur Ada stared up, his eyes red and his tail feathers quivering. "There are too many here now. Too many crows and too many quail. The mice are without end. We are shades for slaughter. We have fattened ourselves until we are grown indolent and smug." Cotur Ada looked to Nascus. "Prince, your father was a wise King, surely, but he was lazy." Nascus furled his brow.

"Oh, the wolf will come," continued Cotur Ada. "And its order will be one of blood and darkness. The crows will be its servants, and in the end, all animals—crows, quail, rabbits, every one—its prey. I beg you hear me. The wolf will come if the hawk does not return."

Ophrei looked deeply into the quail's eyes, and for a moment it was almost as if he had softened and was to concede, to make allowance for the words the quail had spoken. Hidden deep within the brush, Ysil felt a brief surge of hope. But it was short-lasting.

"You speak the ramblings of an old fool, bird," said Ophrei, resolving himself. "You must now suffer for your presence here. You must suffer the Spiking. No animal dare come here today, neither mole nor swallow. Even those birds in migration dare not land when the crows are gathered. The messenger doves are nowhere to be seen. No bat will chase mosquito over this field when the crows are so assembled. All who dare intrude will die and you, old bird, though you have made this field your home the entirety of your life, are no different."

Cotur Ada lowered his head. "Do as your order commands," he said.

* * *

YSIL AND MONROTH watched the happenings in horror. Ysil was overwhelmed. Cotur Ada the father of a hawk? Now the journey the old bird had commanded seemed to take on more meaning. Ysil felt his grandfather's feather tucked within his breast and hoped should they make it to the hawk's realm it would offer protection from his sharp beak.

Ysil understood that the next few moments were to be the last in Cotur Ada's life. He wanted beyond hope for there to be a miracle to save his grandfather, but he was helpless to provide it. All the young quails could do was to sit and watch as fate resolved.

FAR ABOVE IN the blue of the afternoon sky, a tiny speck flew over unnoticed. Zeno the dove knew that to be caught spying on the crows' undisclosed ceremony would bring his death. Flying as high as possible and still low enough to see the forms on the golden field, Zeno counted birds. He barely made out the tiny gray form of a quail. He could never have identified the bird except for the fact he held his head up and was face-to-face with the crows. Only one of the field's quail would have such bravery to yield. Only Cotur Ada. He watched as the small form lowered his head to the crows before him, and at this Zeno knew the bird's fate was sealed.

Zeno turned to the cold wind and flew with all his strength. He would never make it to the Vulture Field before dark and would have to roost the night somewhere. When he felt he was a safe distance from the crows' watch, he flew low along a wooded trail. He saw three quail struggling fast through the late afternoon shadows. He passed on. And when he came to a fork in the trail, he made a detour to a stand of cedar and descended to the den within. He spoke to the woodchuck living there, told him of the goings-on in the field and of the tiny quail on the path. Then he took to air again and forwarded upon a new command, for the woodchuck had whispered his own fears of something new to the dove, and in their exchange the woodchuck relieved the dove of his mission. And the woodchuck, called Risa, set out from the safety of his den to seek out the quail, the struggling older and the two small, to guard them through the night, then bear them to Olffey Field with burdensome news. He would tell them what the dove knew had happened. The crows had killed Cotur Ada, as their order demanded. Perhaps they already knew.

But the woodchuck would have no word of the small quail that were held up in the brush. If asked of them, he would have nothing to offer but the vague speculations of a woodchuck, which were few.

Fragit the General followed the command of Ophrei the rook and made Cotur Ada, the eldest of the quail, to lie down on the field. The old quail did not beg for his life or speak another word.

"Now you will pass your body to the field," said Ophrei. "You have done a foolish thing by coming here, quail. This is a dire day, and it is sad that with all the killing that took place here today we must add another senseless death to the number."

He turned to Fragit. “General, dispatch this quail. Return him to the earth from whence he came. Spike him. Remove his head and place it where all can see, so that those returning will be reminded of the order. Surely none will come again when commanded to stay away.”

The General glared down at the prone form of Cotur Ada. The old quail did not quiver in fear as Fragit would have believed him to. He only lay there, still as if he were already dead, his wings spread wide, his body flat on the ground, eyes closed and head slightly to one side. Fragit leaped upon the quail, his wings hurriedly beating. He stared down at the form of the smaller bird. “You will now die, quail,” was all he said. And with that, he drove his beak into the back of Cotur Ada’s neck, piercing his skin and straight through his spine, killing him instantly.

And thus Cotur Ada, the wisest of the quail, passed from the known world. And because of his noble sacrifice, five quail lived that day. And hidden in the brush, Ysil wept. Monroth shook in fear.

Chapter Seven

Visitors in the Darkness

Ysil and Monroth lay as immobile as their terrified bodies would allow. Ysil told himself there was nothing he could have done to save his beloved grandfather. However, he felt a burden of guilt within his heart. He had been useless and powerless. They watched as Cotur Ada's body was shredded and his head carried away to the Murder's Tree, his skull to be spiked upon a dead branch. From their hiding place they could still see a few of his gray feathers blowing in the wind as the day's light waned and the promise of dusk befell the Murder's Field. The crows one by one returned to their tree in preparation for the night's nesting.

Quail, really most all birds, do not fly at night. The reason is simple: they can't see. Of course, there are some birds that see just fine in the dark. The whippoorwill, the nightingale, and, indeed, the owl. Oh, for the grace of the wind, the owl! Ysil prayed they not see an owl. Surely Strix was not close. He was not welcomed by the crows. But the night was his realm, and how could the crows know if he were to fly through seeking mice or perhaps two little lost quail? However, he felt certain it would be known if Strix had been carousing and hunting. The crows' count of mice would be in descent and he would have heard.

Quail nest at night on the ground and do not move through the descent of darkness, which is when the foxes and coyotes begin to prowl. Tonight, Ysil and Monroth would have no choice. They would have to move away from the field through the gathering dark and get at least a fair distance away before they settled to nest. If they were too close come morning, the crows could see them and suspect they'd secreted a view of the Reckoning; this suspicion would be enough to get them killed.

So they lay there silently until the last crow was gone from the field and evening began to fall over the place they called their home. Then, with as much quiet and stealth as possible, they moved through the brush and away from the field.

Ysil felt certain he could find the trail in the shadows. "It has to be this way!" he called softly to Monroth, gesturing in the direction that he believed Cotur Ada had flown to intersect Banka and Incanta.

"No, Ysil! That is not the way to the path." Monroth was adamant, and not only that. Ysil felt heartlessness in his voice. They had just watched the death of the elder, but now that Monroth's life was no longer in immediate danger, he was prideful. Ysil said nothing about this.

"I know it's this way, Monroth," said Ysil. "I remember seeing Incanta and the two chicks right here." He stamped his foot on the ground. "I'm going this way, and you may as well follow." Ysil set off down the path.

"Well, I am not going that way," said Monroth. "I'll just sit right here for a while, and when you get lost and start crying, I'll come rescue you."

"If you sit for long, you will fall asleep," Ysil whispered back. "We have to get farther away."

Monroth considered this. "All right. I'll follow you. But when we get lost, I will lead from then on." The bigger bird smirked and followed, surely hoping to prove him wrong.

On Ysil led through a batch of thick brush and to a red ash he knew especially well. He had sat perched in the tree just the week before and counted ducks as they flew overhead in groups of two or three. They passed the tree and, within moments, were on the trail.

And though his heart was broken by the loss of his grandfather, Ysil raised his beak to Monroth in triumph, relishing his minor victory.

"I always knew it was here," said Monroth. "I was just testing you."

They went down the trail quickly, and kept moving, though inevitably twilight came. They forged on, fighting the instinct for sleep, pushing through the dense undergrowth of fanworts, broom sedge, musk thistle, and red sorrel. And still they continued, stumbling at times over rocks and roots exposed, beneath the darkening green canopy. They pressed through the forest with sleep beckoning them like Mother from her late spring nest.

GOMOR AND CORMO were still and quiet at the descent of night. They had seen but a few small songbirds and no other creatures. Gomor was a bit worried about leaving his family without telling them of his adventurous plans, but of course the young will be young and neither bird nor rabbit worried too much. After all, they would see their families tomorrow, assuredly. They wanted to make an early meeting with Ysil, Cotur Ada, and Monroth. And certainly not long after that the whole of the field dwellers would be going back home.

But for now they settled down beneath the shelter of a willow in the recess of the fallen tree Cormo had seen earlier in the day and lay still.

Then they heard the voice.

"Oh, boys, I hear your whispering," came the soft call. It was Harlequin. She sounded playful, but there was unrestrained relief in her voice. "Am I glad I found you," she said.

"Over here!" called out Gomor, a bit too loud for Cormo. "We are here!"

They heard her rustling then curse softly, missing a step and tripping. She moved through the shadowy undergrowth, careful of her footing, and settled close to Gomor. She'd had a kinship with the rabbit since they were young, and he, of course, adored her as a dear friend.

"Well, well," she said. "If I haven't found my brave young adventurers. Let's keep company."

"Why on earth would you follow us? You are crazy to move through these woods alone!" said Cormo, but even as he said this he remembered what he had overheard her tell Cotur Mono and knew: Monroth. She wanted to find Monroth.

"Well," she said, "I couldn't let you two take off by yourselves and have all the fun. And besides, you need someone to take care of you."

It was nearly dark now.

Gomor huffed. "And you would be that one? Really!" He lay still.

All this talk and Cormo was a bit nervous. "Be quiet, you two. Remember the rules of the wood at night. We must stay quiet."

They fell silent. Harlequin rustled a bit closer to Cormo, and he felt her feathers brush his. He shivered. Harlequin was his cousin and he had never carried Harlequin within his heart, but being this close to her and her immediate need for his presence was flattering to him. She was unquestionably as tense as they were about being alone in the forest and certainly a good measure more afraid than she sounded, facing the prospect of sleeping by herself with the dangers of night about. Surely she had never done that before. She would in no doubt be huddling this close to any of the covey, or any rabbit for that matter.

And so they settled down, and with dark closing fast, the two quail fell asleep. Gomor lay there listening only for a moment, then began to rummage through the surrounding leaves looking for something to eat.

"WAKE UP!" THERE came a voice to Cormo like one within a dream, and he fought the web of sleep to reply.

"What is it, Gomor?" said Cormo, his mind tangled within a night's dreams.

"There is something near!" whispered Gomor.

Then he heard it. The undeniable rush of great wings. His heart seized in his chest at that sound as only the prey can. He spun around to Gomor, who was staring into the black, his eyes attuned to darkness.

Gomor looked over to Harlequin, who had awoken also. She had lowered her head to the ground, her eyes wide and frightened. The rush of wings within the descending dark of night could mean only one thing: an owl.

They all huddled still. Had the bird heard them talking? It could have been nesting in a nearby tree and they would never have known. Then the rush sounded again and they knew the bird was falling down toward them. With a great final flurry of wings, the great bird settled upon the fallen tree inches above their nest.

"Who?" called a voice deep and grand. "Who, my little morsels, are you?"

"I THINK WE are far enough away now to bed down," said Monroth.

"We should go farther," said Ysil. "With the chaos of the day, some crows may have ventured out of the field to make nest. May even be some nesting across the ridge we just descended." He trudged on through the relative darkness. Monroth huffed but followed.

Then from ahead they heard the unquestionable sound of voices.

"Wake up!" came a familiar voice from the wooded brushy area just beyond the bend. Gomor! Ysil wanted to call out but was nervous in the dark. Instinct kept them quiet.

Then, "What is it, Gomor?" Ysil's heart leaped. It was Cormo!

They moved on silently for a few paces then heard the swoop of wings. There was not even a thought of what it might be. It was the owl.

Ysil saw it beat its wings and dive to the ground. Close, dreadfully close. Then he heard the voice of the owl, sounding dark and hungry. "Who? Who, my little morsels, are you?"

A stark terror settled in Ysil's belly like an eagle's talon. But it was not a terror that froze him in place. Ysil was suddenly thinking of nothing but the fact his dearest friends were certainly beneath the talons of the owl. He thrashed his wings and flew at the sound of the voice with all he had.

"Scatter!" Ysil screamed with all his might, flushing feverously toward the sound of the voices.

Two birds flew at his command. The second was Harlequin. The rabbit jumped also. They instinctively went in three different directions. Ysil felt relief in the fact that his friends had fled, but the owl was still sitting there. It had hardly moved a feather when Ysil screamed. Then he saw two great orbs that were the eyes of the owl staring directly at him, watching the fast-approaching form of a small quail dive-bombing him in crazed suicidal flight. Looking up to an easy meal. It was only then that Ysil realized the folly in his flight of rescue. He had not thought; he had just reacted.

Ysil swerved drastically in his approach, to alter his perceived attack to an escape. Below, the owl raised its great wings and made preparations, opening its pointed beak, the red tongue extending to taste the air. When the owl perceived that Ysil was off course from his original approach, it took to wing in pursuit. Ysil heard a flurry to his tail and realized that Monroth was behind. The other bird must have reacted quickly when Ysil flew. *Perhaps he saw Harlequin*, thought Ysil. He had barely enough time to feel a slight surprise before they both crashed noisily into the brush. Then the great form of the owl was at the brush right behind them. Ysil and Monroth froze still on the ground. The owl poked its beak in and glared into the dark of the brush, staring directly at the quail. But it did not try to push its huge body within the thorny brambles. Ysil and Monroth were motionless.

There was a flutter of great wings and then the owl was gone. As it flew, it let out a great laugh. Ysil would have thought the laugh to say, *I will get you soon*, but there was something different in it. There was something that said, *What a joy!* Or even, *That was fantastically funny!* This tone of the owl's laughter confused and bewildered Ysil, who realized this was entertaining to the owl.

Beside him, Monroth huddled in fear. They were as still as possible. In a few minutes the excitement abated and the night took over, both around them and within their bodies. And within the hovel of the bush the quail closed their eyes, exhaustion overtaking them. Before long the two were asleep. Mere feet away, Cormo and Harlequin slept also.

Only Gomor was awake, afraid and shivering.

Quail, he thought. *No matter what the day holds, the quail sleep. How can a quail sleep when the owl was just so close?* But when dark fell, quail slept.

YSIL AWOKE TO the sound of laughter. He knew the voice. He would not normally say that a voice like that would make him feel better, but it was a playful sound, a fun-loving laugh. His mind cleared a bit, and then he knew who it was: Drac.

"So, my little quail!" sneered the fox. "You were under attack last night, eh? We were close and heard the bird fly. What a show you put on! I would have thought he would have eaten at least one of your tender bodies! He could have, you know. He must not have been very hungry. What luck! The next time you will not find such luck, eh? You need someone to watch over you. Little quailsies and a tiny rabbit have no place in these big woods alone, no place at all."

Ysil was lying still. Early morning light was sifting through the leaves and an easy wind blew the willow above. From their brambly bed it was Monroth who spoke first: "We don't need taken care of! If you were close and you wanted to help, why didn't you jump to our aid when the owl attacked? And besides, we can fend for ourselves!" Monroth moved out of the brush and walked up to the foxes, face-to-face.

"I do not believe you, little bird!" said Drac. "We would have come to your aid if that owl had gotten hold of you. But when we saw that you made it to the copse, we said to each other, 'Let them sleep.' And we could hardly keep our laughter."

Ysil moved out of the thicket and joined Monroth. "Monroth, we shouldn't even be talking to them. Remember what Cotur Ada said? Please, let's go on."

Monroth opened his beak to speak, but before he could, a voice came from behind: "And how can we trust that you will not eat us yourselves when we sleep?" It was Harlequin.

"Well, well," said Puk. "What a pretty thing you are!"

"Now, Puk, be polite," said Drac. "Let's make them feel more comfortable. Now, are you not hungry? We have, um, already eaten this morning."

"What exactly did you eat?" asked Ysil. "Our cousin's eggs, maybe?"

"Ysil!" hushed Monroth.

Drac gave a toothy smile in response.

Harlequin demanded to be heard. "As I said, how can we be sure you will not eat us, if we allow you to come with us and protect us?"

Come with us? thought Ysil. Then he realized she was thinking of the short journey back to the Vulture Field. She did not know that he and Monroth must be off for a much longer journey.

"You have my word as a fox!" said Drac.

Harlequin smiled. "What kind of word is that? I would prefer the word of a weasel!"

"Surely you must jest, chick. A fox's word is as good as the earth, eh, Drac?" said Puk.

"The best I can do for now, my lovely one, is to point the way to a patch of berries we just chanced upon where you can feed." Drac pulled up tall. "'Twas the berries we ate, yes it was. I can promise you this: Stay close to us when you travel the woods, and you need not fear. We will always lead you to food. Now, go down that small path there"— he pointed an outstretched claw to a break in the tree line—"and once you reach a dead hickory, walk just ten paces into the forest behind it. There you will find the berry bush. You go there and talk, make your decision, and we will be on in just a bit."

The foxes romped off into the woods, leaving the others no time to respond.

"Well," said Gomor, "I for one am hungry enough to steal honey from a bear this morning." And with that he jumped off down the trail.

The others stared at one another for a moment, and when none of them spoke, they took off in pursuit of the rabbit.

AND SO, AS they walked, Ysil and Monroth told Harlequin, Gomor, and Cormo what had happened to Cotur Ada. Harlequin cried, for she loved the old quail especially.

"He was extraordinarily brave," said Ysil.

Monroth flushed. "We should have gone to his aid, Ysil. You should have listened to me."

"Oh? And what could we have done?" Ysil asked. "And I don't remember you saying a word about going to his aid. You know very well if we had, we would be dead now also."

Harlequin looked up at Monroth in tears. "I could not stand to lose you both also! Don't mention it."

Monroth looked down at the forest floor.

They continued on a bit until they saw the dead hickory, just as the foxes had promised. They padded silently behind it, not knowing what to expect (except for Monroth, who insisted the foxes were not lying. "Why would they?" he asked. Ysil shivered at the thought), but there it was—a gigantic blackberry bush, laden with late season berries, some dried up, but mostly sweet and tasty—and not many turned sour.

Monroth hopped over to the bush and began eating. "What did I tell you? They will be fine guardians. I do not intend on telling them this, but I will feel quite a bit safer at night with them close."

"Why would we need them to guard us back to the vultures' field, Monroth?" asked Harlequin.

Gomor and Cormo only listened thus far. They watched Monroth intently. The bird gave up nothing, just kept eating.

"Well, Cotur Ada gave us a command," said Ysil. "We aren't going to meet up with the others. Not just yet."

"What do you mean?" questioned Gomor. "Why wouldn't you?"

"Well," began Ysil, though he did not know just how to finish.

"Ysil's grandfather commanded that we should go and find

his son." It was Monroth who said this, his beak dark purple and thick with the gore of berries.

Cormo responded: "You are speaking nonsense. Cotur Ada has no surviving sons that I know of, only grandchicks."

"Apparently, there is one . . . " said Ysil, trailing off.

"And the one is a hawk, it seems," said Monroth.

Harlequin, Gomor, and Cormo looked at the two birds as if they had lost their minds.

And so Ysil related Cotur Ada's song to the others, or at least the tale within it, and when he finished, Monroth was sitting against a small hackberry, his belly full. "So now you can see why we should take on the guardianship of the foxes. Surely they already know of our destination," said Monroth. "They must know of whom we seek and that if he returns to the field, they should be in his favor. As our friends, they would find this."

"What in earth are you talking about?" said Cormo. "The damned foxes don't think we will befriend the hawk. More than likely they think we will be eaten by it, and that maybe they can gather our bones for spoils."

"If that is true, then why don't they eat us now?" said Ysil.

The others stared at Ysil. This was the first sign he had made of accepting the foxes' guardianship.

"Are you suggesting that we allow them to protect us?" asked Harlequin.

"Perhaps there is some wisdom in it," said Ysil. "I must allow, if they wanted to kill us, they likely would have done so by now."

"Wait a moment. You are not going with us, Harlequin," said Monroth.

"Why, yes, I am," she answered.

"This journey is not for you," said Ysil.

"And why not, Ysil?" answered Harlequin. "Did I not love him also? Was he not my grandfather's best friend? I will let you and Monroth be the ones to speak with the hawk, that is certain, but I will go with you on your journey."

"Well, I for one have been hoping for a true adventure since we left for Olffey!" It was Gomor. "It seems this will be just that!"

Ysil paid no mind to the rabbit but kept his attentions upon Harlequin. "But you cannot go!" he said. "You would not be safe."

"Let her come if she pleases," said Monroth. "I will care for her."

"Well, we can all care for her," said Ysil, stammering.

"Wait a moment," said Harlequin. "I don't need anyone caring for me. I'll take care of myself!"

"Oh, we will care for you all," came the voice from the other side of the berry bush. "We will care for you as if you were our own cubs." And with that, Drac and Puk came out from the brambles with an easy and silent gait, almost as if they had been listening there all along. And when Ysil thought on it for a moment, he decided that they had.

AND SO IT was decided that the two foxes would accompany the group as far as the Great River.

"What will we owe you in return?" asked Ysil.

"We will ask of you nothing, young one," said Drac. "Only that you allow us your favor in days to come."

"Exactly what does that mean?" asked Gomor. He had noticed that Puk would on occasion look down at his muscled legs with an awkward and strange look in his eye. He didn't like it.

"It means, my rabbit friend, that you will not be a party to the crows' way of keeping us from the field once the new order is established, see?" Drac kept his teeth exposed as he talked. "That if things should change and the crows lose power, we be allowed to rid the area of wasps and hornets, that we be allowed to keep the population of mice at bay. That you four, at least, will hold closer allegiance to our kind, and not hinder our hunting. Of course, we will leave your eggs alone."

Ysil was having trouble believing the fox, but he did not voice this. "So you know of our journey," said Ysil. "You know of our plans to ask Pitrin to return to the field?"

Drac smiled. "We are the ears of the forest, young bird. If it is spoken in the quiet of the woods, consider it as given that a fox has heard."

"I am telling you that the foxes are good to have along," said Monroth. "And these two we can trust. As I said, they know that times are changing."

Drac smiled at Monroth and showed his long and sharp canines. It appeared to Ysil that some sort of communication passed between them, and if he didn't know better, he would have thought that Monroth winked one feathered eyelid.

Then the rest of the birds and the rabbit ate from the berry bush until they were full. The foxes sat near and preened their fur.

A robin chanced upon the animals and briefly perched in the tree above the bush. She gazed in wonder at the strange group below and thought to herself, *What is this forest coming to?* Then she ruffled her feathers and took wing, hoping to find tasty worms in the compost of a different berry bush.

Chapter Eight

The King of the Forest

ASMOD THE WOLF breathed in the forest. He owned the forest as he did his own tail, his darkly stained fur, and his claws. He knew the forest as the reading of a possum's entrails, as the lines of mud left from melting snow. The forest was his, just as certainly as the teeth in his mouth or his single eye.

He had not always owned just the forest. When he was younger, the pack held the field and the forest both. The pack was as one. He was within the pack and he hunted with them. They were of the same order, an unstoppable force of gnashing fangs and muscle, bound together by common hunger and lust. Oh, the lust of the pack. He shuddered when the thought came. He remembered as a pup being led into the field where a group of woodchucks were surrounded. Within the pack were his mother and father, and his older brothers and sisters, eight of them. The pack fell upon the woodchucks, and so did he. And so his first kill had been an old gray woodchuck, slow and feeble. He still held the memory dear, and it comforted him like a lover through the night. He treasured the lust for the kill, which was forever his, and he cherished the memories of the pack. But the lust of the pack never would be again. The pack members were all dead.

He was the only survivor of his litter. A man had chanced upon him and his siblings while his mother was hunting with the older ones. The man had put them in a box and carried them to a pond. When he opened the box and looked in at them, he grabbed all the others and pushed them into a sack, but Asmod had bitten him, then jumped and ran. The man cursed and tied the sack shut—after filling it with rocks. Asmod remembered the cries of his brothers and sisters, how they had called out for help, how some had called his name, and he remembered how their cries had abruptly stopped when the man had thrown the bag into the water.

He hated men. He swore someday that he would kill the man who had done that; he would rip out his throat.

He remembered how the crows had sworn their allegiance to the wolves, how they had promised to work with them to herd in the mice and rabbits, how they would always respect the wolves. And when the man had come into the field and laid out poison meats and killed many of his family, the crows had merely watched as the wolves ate the meat. And though they had seen the man's treachery during the daylight hours, they had not warned the wolves of the poison and had slept through their feast of polluted flesh. He remembered how they had laughed as his older brothers and sisters had died, how they rested safely in the branches above as his father and uncles had cursed them, while his mother had cried. He hated crows for that. He had vowed to kill every crow he could catch. He would kill them, slowly and painfully.

And he remembered how the hawk Elera had flown down on him as he was feasting on a fallen chick from her nest. He recalled a screeching descent and the feeling of her beak piercing his eyeball, making a resounding *pop*, and then the feeling of the eye being pulled from the socket, the pain, the sound of her screams mixed with his own howls of agony. He hated hawks. He would kill any hawk he ever encountered.

And he remembered how the men had come together with their dogs and had run the remainder of the pack into the woods and cornered them in the darkness of Vangly Cave. He had hidden still in the back, covered in the thick, black mud, while the pack fought the dogs. He would never forget how the men had come with great lights and the horrible booms of their sticks, the deafening echoes off the cave walls—the screams of his family dying. He had lain still, the blood of his family too strong in the dogs' noses to catch the scent of one last survivor. The men dragged the wolf bodies out into the dark night. He stayed hidden all the next day and ventured out only when the sun descended. When he came out of the cave he smelled meat cooking. Then he had seen the fire. He approached and his stomach turned in hunger. But the meat was charred skeletons. It was his family burned on a great pyre.

He had run into the forest and kept running. He had run until he came to a great river, then swam across it. He had not stopped until he reached a cliff at the base of a white-topped mountain. He crawled into a den there, wet and cold to the middle of his body. In the dark he felt an icy slithering beneath his belly. Then he felt the teeth sink in.

The snake smiled at him and said, "Oh, but I am sorry, great wolf. I did not see it was you before I bit. I see you are weak. May I have your warmth until you die?" He let the copperhead curl up next to him, ready for the end. He had grown deathly ill, but, for some fated reason, he did not die. In his recovery the wolf heard tales from the great snake of a band of crows that had picked into his nest and killed his mate and slithery children. The wolf and snake developed a friendship; they hunted together through that spring. The wolf brought the snake mice and rabbits, while the snake would poison bigger prey, prey too big for the wolf to bring down without the help of the pack. They hunted together not unlike the pack itself. Though Tortrix could never keep up with him, the snake could get into places that Asmod could not. He would crawl silently into a badger's den and bite the animal in its sleep. When the badger woke in agony and thirst and crept from its den, Asmod would be waiting outside. Though at first the wolf grew ill upon consuming the bodies of the poisoned prey, over time he grew immune to the snake's venom. They grew strong and fat together, and all the other animals feared and respected them. The snake grew accustomed to wrapping itself around the wolf's neck. And they ruled the forest together.

It was a difficult relationship at times, but it was their common goal that kept the snake and wolf together—their lust for the kill. Together, they were more successful than they ever were alone.

Asmod seldom thought of the pack anymore, but on nights when the moon was full and he felt the need rising within him like a consuming fire he would call out an anguished howl, hoping that someday, someway, he would be answered back. But the answer never came. It was a lonely echo that returned to him. And deep within he knew that he was the last of his kind, and that only the silent orb of the moon was his true kin.

ON THIS DAY, Asmod was awakened at dusk by first the smell of, and then the sound of, an approaching snake. The belly of a legless one moving across the forest floor was not easy to hear, and most who had the ears to hear it could not say what the sound was. But Asmod had become comfortably familiar with it. Tortrix was near, curled and sleeping, so he knew it was not him. Then the sound doubled, then tripled, and he thought to himself, *Visitors, eh?* He could hear their bellies' scaled skins moving stealthily across the pine needles until they were at the edge of the den, just past its opening within a small stand of trees. He lay still and opened his one dark eye. His fur was black, stained with drying blood. It wasn't until he sensed that they were at the very mouth of the den that he made a move at all. Then he slowly raised his head.

They did not see the wolf, cloaked in darkness. He heard one of them speaking in hushed tones: "Ssssso, I tell you we should leave now! He would just as soon eat us as listen to ussssss!"

"He will lissssten," said another. "When he hearsssss what we have to tell, he will lisssten! The King of the Crows is dead and a great time is upon ussss! They are in chaos in the field! So much blood to fill our bellies delicioussssly soon. He will thank ussss."

At this Asmod stepped into the light, into the very midst of the intruders. The snakes—a massasauga, a young copperhead, and a thick timber rattlesnake—froze at the appearance of the enormous monster. "What is that you say? The King of the Crows is dead? Do you not know, fools? As soon as the King dies, there is a choosing of a new King." Asmod rose taller on his paws. "Certainly their order is strong. Now away with you! Before I devour your loathsome flesh as early breakfast!"

"Yesssss . . . " came the voice from the still coil that was Tortrix. "Leave, you idiots. He will kill you, and I will laugh through my own fangs as his rip you up."

"O wise and great Asmod, we ask you to hear ussss!" nervously called the young copperhead. "Was early this morning that I was at the lake near the man's road. I was looking for duck chicksss and the like when a number of geese flew into the pond. They were talking of the death of the King. But that would not have caused our coming to see you. They ssssaid that the oldest of brothers grew angered when his younger brother was chosen as King. He flew before he could be subdued. He flew away and there is no new King crowned. No King Crow at all, now. The field is in disssorder and confusion!"

Asmod raised his eyebrows at this. "Hmm. And where are these geese now?" he asked.

"They are gone, O fearsssome one! They flew fast after I heard them relating this tale to one another. I waited there for a while, but when I told the massasauga and the other copperheads of what I heard, they sssssaid we must tell you. We all feared you would kill ussss, but we know of your story, as was told by Tortrix in the spring when we were in mate." At this Asmod glared at his companion copperhead, raising his head in a huff. *So*, thought Asmod, *so he has been talking, eh? Must have been to impress the mate* . . . But he let this go. For now.

"And so, what do you think I am to do?" asked the great wolf. "What to do with this knowledge? If I am to return, do you think I would take you with me as my army? A few snakes and one wolf? We may take the field, perhaps, but the hawk will take you all. I am rich here; why would I leave?"

The snakes looked to one another. It was the young rattlesnake that spoke. "O great one, it is not only the news of the King's death we bring. The geese spoke of something else. It has been fourteen seasons since you have been to the field, yes?"

The wolf scowled at him. "Yes, I do admit it has been that long," he said. *Maybe I should kill them after all,* thought Asmod.

"The hawk Elera has been dead for sssix seasonssss," said the young copperhead. "This also the geese spoke of." At this Tortrix uncoiled and raised his head tall, looking at Asmod.

"And what of her children?" asked Asmod.

"They are also dead," said the intruding copperhead.

Asmod stood still in shocked response. Then he turned to Tortrix. "Is your belly full, my friend?"

"Yessss," answered the copperhead. "But I am sure I could eat."

They turned to the snakes with dangerous smiles.

"Not an army, that is for certain," said Asmod.

"Oh, but ssssir!" cried the copperhead. "We have you one ready." And with that the snake made a grunting, seething noise, which was a call of sorts.

The wolf raised his nose to the air. And again Asmod smelled then heard the approach from the surrounding woods. He heard the coming of many small paws and more slithering and the waddle of lizards and the pad of a good few larger paws. He heard them from far away, but they came quickly. Then the smells became thick, the animals in droves. His jaws widened and he began to pant as the first of them entered his bay. There were foxes and coyotes, there were some large timber rattlesnakes and skinks and garter snakes. There were weasels, minks, and two bobcats. They gathered around the wolf, and all of them bowed down to him. They all kept their eyes down and paid respect to the greatest of predators, the greatest of their kind and the last of his own. Then, there at the edge of the forest, Asmod saw another shape, dark and large, hidden behind the laurel, and he smiled when he smelled this thing, for this particular creature had never contributed allegiance to him, though now its mere presence was granting such.

And Asmod rose up tall on his hind legs and laughed, and the laugh turned to a shrill howl and echoed off the trees and the cliff behind him, and the sound fell as it went, but the howl was heard far away. And all who heard it cowered in fear, for it was a howl of triumphant bloodlust.

HIGH ABOVE THE river in a nest of oak twigs and sycamore branches, Pitrin the hawk heard the cry and wondered at it. He knew it to be the wolf, but he, for one, was not afraid, only curious. And in the gathering heat of the day, the great bird took to wing and flew into the heavens, and there upon high he listened to the sound of the wolf's howl echoing across the sky and heard the words hidden within. And the words clouded Pitrin's heart. And there, the fear was finally conceived, for he understood the words.

"I am coming home!" the wolf cried upon the wind.

Chapter Nine

An Invitation and the Journey to the River

MORNING CAME TO the vultures' field. The stillness was not broken by the sound of birds or even by the squawks of the vultures. All was quiet. Cotur Mono found it unnerving that the field was so still, as if it were a great dead thing itself. Why was the early morning not filled with the sound of the waking townhees and warblers that inhabited the woods surrounding? He sat for a long time beneath the lengthy shadow of a fallen sycamore branch, considering the course his kind should take. With each passing moment, there was more of the morning lost. If he were to return on the same route they had taken to this field, it would take all day, an exhausting trip. He did know of a second route, but it would bring the group dangerously close to the man's farm. The man had dogs and the dogs would most certainly smell them. This could be fatally perilous. Still, they could move through in small groups, all staying within a call's distance, and the birds could go first, before the rabbits and mice. That way, if the dogs came, they could take to the air and warn the others of the attack. Cotur Mono sat in the utter silence of the morning considering this, lost in his thoughts.

"Good morning, cousin bird," said a voice right in his ear, and the quail jumped in such a panic he was taken to wing before he realized who it was that had spoken. The leader quail settled back down beside the great vulture with a *hhmmff* and a slight whistle.

"Why are you vultures always so quiet?" asked Cotur Mono. "You scared me to still my heart."

"I am sorry, cousin bird," said the great vulture mother Ekbeth. "I will try to be louder in my approach next time." She smiled and breathed out a sigh. The leader quail could smell death on her breath, could see its black decay smeared throughout her feathers. He quivered.

"Mother!" cried the vulture perched at the highest top of the great dead sycamore. "There comes on approach a woodchuck! And on its back are three small birds!"

"Oh, please," said Cotur Mono. "Let it be some of the misplaced!"

"Certainly it is," said Ekbeth.

The old gray hare Sulari hopped out from beneath the stump where he had slept. "What's that?" he said. "The approach of birds? What type?" He called this to the vulture perched on high.

"Appear to be two tiny quail and one larger, frail and thin—very old. They are climbing down off the woodchuck's back."

By this time the animals were coming out from their sleeping places in curiosity. "Three of the lost ones!" called one voice. "Who is it coming?" called another.

Cotur Mono, Ekbeth, Sulari, and the rest of those awakened by the arrival hurried to the edge of the field to see three quail perched upon the back of a sleek woodchuck. Two were the young lost chicks. The third bird was Incanta.

Sulari and Cotur Mono went straightaway to the old quail, but the young ones flew immediately to their mother, who took them under her wings, crying and preening them. Then she began to peck and scold them for running away. That did not last long, and soon she was preening them and crying again.

Incanta, in exhaustion, sat down. "I may never rise again," she said.

"Mother, I must away," said the woodchuck.

"Thank you, Risa," said Incanta. "If it were not for the dove sending you to us, we would still be on our journey next moon. Bless your swift feet."

"I am honored to carry you. Though the burden of the news you bear is greater in weight than your small bodies." Sulari raised his ears to this. "May peace stay with you, Mother. May your worst days be behind you," said the woodchuck, whose eyes darted nervously about the field, from vulture to quail and back again. He made a sort of deliberate curtsy then, in a flash of brown fur, was gone.

Cotur Mono came close to her. "Incanta, wise hen, I beseech you, why are you the one to return with these young ones?" he asked. "What danger has come to the others?"

"Cotur Ada is dead," she said. Then she went on to tell how he had sacrificed himself, and how she had fled with the chicks as Banka took Cotur Ada into the field. She explained how Risa the woodchuck had come to them not long after they fled, how he had sheltered them throughout the night and delivered them swiftly to Olffey Field come morning.

Cotur Mono cried when he heard of the death of Cotur Ada, and he pulled a footful of feathers from his breast, casting them on the wind.

"What of the others?" queried Sulari, likewise distraught. "What of Harlequin, Gomor, and Cormo? What of Ysil and Monroth?"

"I saw nothing of them," she said.

Cotur Mono opened his beak and, looking to Sulari for support, said, "I can only hope they escaped before they were found by the crows, but I fear they may not have been so fortunate."

Cotur Mono fell into a thoughtful silence as all around the animals chattered excitedly. Anur was telling of how Banka had held him and his small brother down, and that he was certain he would die; that they both would be dead if it weren't for Cotur Ada and Incanta.

The vultures' field was filled with chatter and excited talk. Some wanted to flee the area, to not return to the field. All were extremely angry at the crows for the murder. Some questioned if Cotur Ada had really been murdered at all. Sulari assured them that he had. "The little ones saw the crows kill a prince within the order of their Reckoning," said the old gray hare. "Why would they likewise not slaughter a mere quail?" None dared speak of revenge. The dark happenings of the Reckoning were beyond the understanding of the lesser animals, but from what they had heard, it was an evil thing. Incanta told Sulari of the flight of the prince and his followers. Sulari asked many questions, but through this Cotur Mono spoke not a word.

Then the leader of the quail flew up to a low branch on the sycamore where all could see him and, gathering up his spirit, said, "The crows have murdered one of our own; yes, it is devastating. I, as much as any of you, am greatly angered upon hearing this. But know that Cotur Ada knew his path when he made his choice. He gave his life for these young ones and for Incanta. This is the greatest love." All were quiet.

He continued. "We should all hold what he did as the highest of acts. Let us not focus on his murder, for the crows are only following the ancient laws laid down within their order. They are no more to blame for his death than the rain drowning newborn mice within the den." At this there was a consenting murmur through the group.

And then from the back came a voice seldom heard, that of Roe the golden rat. "Well, their order is not ours. Should we not consider this?"

"Cotur Mono speaks with wisdom," said Sulari. "We cannot challenge their order. We need only tend to our own."

"Eh?" spoke Incanta, resting on the barren earth, belabored with heavy breath. "I challenged only to try to save the hatchlings. And I am old, as was Cotur Ada. But I feel he was bound by a decision beyond his personal sacrifice. I feel he had something to say. I pray he had the chance to say it before his life was taken."

"What was he to say?" asked Cotur Mono. "What message would he have for the crows?"

"Cotur Ada knew of the unbalance in the field," she said. "He knew that there are missing pieces to the life therein. He knew that he would have their ear. There could never be another time when he would."

Sulari and Cotur Mono pondered this for a moment. Then Cotur Mono raised his voice to the group. "We are going home today." There was an unsettled murmur. Ekbeth nodded her head.

"We will help you prepare passage to the field, animals. And we will gather acorns for you this morning so that you are fed before your journey." Her massive beak wide open, she made her last offer: "And remember, our offer is always open. Any of you are welcome to remain here."

"I am staying," said Incanta.

"What?" cried Sulari and Cotur Mono at once.

"I swore not to make the journey, but since I had no choice and I am here anyway, I am staying. I knew that if I came I could never leave." She smiled at Ekbeth. "You have a place for an old, flightless quail here, Mother Vulture?"

"Certainly we do, wise one!" Ekbeth was honored and excited. "You may share the north end of the field with the elder deer and the coyote. Certainly you will have much to talk about. Where else can you glean such wisdom but here?"

"I am awfully eager," said Incanta. "I have much to ask them, most certainly the coyote."

As they saw her resolve, Sulari and Cotur Mono did not argue with her. They gathered around Incanta and pressed in close to her. Cotur Mono laid his wings on her and Sulari, his arms. The leader quail prayed for her there, prayed to the wind, and the hare even said a prayer to the earth. They prayed she would continue to learn and find wisdom even in that place of dying. Then she walked silently to the far end of the field, where the coyote and deer watched her approach with interest. She sat down between them.

The animals began to prepare for the journey back. And the vultures came with branches filled with acorns, and they all ate well. Before the morning sun had reached one quarter, the group took to the trail, heading home.

From the north end of the field, Incanta watched the others leave. She nuzzled her head into the soft fur of the coyote and closed her eyes. With great care the coyote whispered softly into her ear. "Sleep, Mother," he said.

WITH EVERY STEP Ysil took, his mistrust for the honesty and forthrightness of their 'guardians' grew. He watched their every move and was forever reminding himself to be ready to take flight should they turn from protectors to attackers.

Drac had insisted that he be at the front of the group, to lead and to confront anyone they might encounter. If a foe were to be moving down the trail during the light of day, surely a fox was a better initial encounter than a quail or a rabbit. But if another quail were moving down the trail, or a rabbit or a raccoon even, they would see the approach of a fox. The word of a group of prey moving with predators would spread quickly if a dove were to see them. If he encountered a dove, what would he say? *The foxes are here to take us to the river where we intend on asking the hawk to return to the field*? Any dove would think them crazed. *Will this be before or after they eat you?* the dove might ask.

Puk was at the rear of the group to fend off any danger from behind. Ysil hated the thought of their flanks being exposed to the fox. He felt the fox's eyes on him and kept glancing back, imagining hunger within them.

"You need not get too far from the others now," Ysil heard Puk say to Gomor, who had fallen behind. "Someone may eat you."

Ysil shivered. Gomor laughed uneasily. "Thanks for your consideration," he said.

Monroth had taken to walking beside Drac, and though the fox had cautioned him against it, he had continued to do so. "I want to be close should we need to protect Harlequin," he said, looking back to see if she heard.

Ysil glanced at Harlequin. Her feathers ruffled slightly and a light came to her eyes. Ysil grimaced.

They had been moving all day and decided to stop in a small clearing, hoping to find some food. The foxes took to tearing apart an old dead tree stump, looking for grubs and ants. The rest pecked and foraged around the field for what greenery and seed they could find.

Harlequin moved close to Ysil. He trembled.

"What do you think, Ysil?" she asked. "Do you think we can trust them? Any at all?"

"I think we can trust them to look out for their own needs," said Ysil. "They must think there is something important in it for them to be with us. I don't think it's to put us in their bellies. Not right away, at least. If they just wanted to eat us, they would have tried by now."

"You're right, and there are certainly dangers always about," she said. "Have you ever been this far in the direction the sun rises before?"

Ysil shook his head. "No, and neither have Cormo nor Gomor. I don't know about Monroth—he has made a few journeys. For all I know, he may have been down this very trail with the foxes themselves."

"Do you really think so?" she asked with sudden interest. "Has he really taken such journeys?"

"Oh, I don't know, probably not this far," said Ysil.

Then the laughter started. It was all around the clearing.

The laughter was familiar, and even before the furry masks appeared out of the bush Ysil knew who it was that was raising the ruckus: raccoons, pesky and noisome raccoons. Ysil, Cormo, and Harlequin moved together. Monroth immediately gathered in with them. He pushed into the middle. Ysil saw him shudder, and he pressed himself up beside Harlequin.

"Ho! What is this?" called the one first into the clearing. Drac moved to face it straight on. "Are you foxes feeding your dinner to fatten it up before you feast? These are such tasty morsels, certainly!" Raccoon were hunters, for sure, but they ate mostly eggs, crawfish, and the occasional shrew. Ysil had never heard of a raccoon killing a live quail or a rabbit. Still, he didn't like the sound of this coon's voice.

"Step back, coon," said Puk, moving to Drac's side. "These are under our care. They are on a great journey, and we will protect them to the river."

"Protect them?" another of the raccoons said, laughing. "From whom? I would make the wager that you foxes need more care yourselves."

"Hmm," mumbled Drac under his breath. "It is best that you be on your way."

"What say, brothers?" said one raccoon. "What be best for us? Could be, fox, that we want those grubs you are into."

"Pass on, you masked trickster," said Drac. "We know you are never in for a fight. Not unless you're cornered. Be on your way."

Then the raccoons all laughed at once as if on cue and began running about the field. Ysil's concern for the coon's intentions dwindled when he heard the words of their song:

What say dance?
Shall we dance to the night?
Shall I chomp on your tail with teeth sharp and white?

What say laugh?
Shall we laugh at the rain?
Shall I bite on your ear while you yelp in pain?

What say jump! (And with this the raccoons made a mighty leap into the air.)
Shall we jump at the sun?
Shall we gulp its fire up just for fun?

What say sleep?
You are so far from home.
Take a good rest while we munch up your bones!

While we munch up your bones!
While we munch up your bones!
While we munch up your bones!
While we munch up . . .

And singing their merry song, the raccoons skipped and bounded off into the woods, their song and laughter ringing through the golden leaves of the trees.

Gomor turned to Ysil. "This is certainly turning out to be an interesting companionship with the foxes," he whispered.

"And quite a journey. Those raccoons wouldn't have stopped us at all if the foxes had not been here."

"Pay no attention to the coons," said Puk. "They are but clowns." He had heard Gomor, though he was across the clearing.

"What we may attract will be of no harm to you," said Drac. "What we will fend off is of dire concern."

"You are right," said Monroth. "Gomor, those raccoons are of no worry and I always knew it. Why, just last week I spent the afternoon with one at the spring. I helped him turn over rocks to find crawfish."

Cormo rolled his eyes and Ysil smiled back. Then he caught Monroth watching and saw the boastful bird had noted the exchange. Monroth scowled at Ysil but said nothing, though Ysil saw in Monroth's eye at that moment something he had never seen before. He was used to the bird's boasting and pride, but here was something dangerous and hateful.

Monroth moved over next to Drac. "Let's go," he said to the fox.

"As you wish, Master Quail," said the fox with a toothy, ravenous grin.

Chapter Ten

The Bonds of Outcasts

"THERE IS A thunder coming!" called Meeki the rebel scout. Sintus looked up from the mouse carcass he was eating and stared. "There is a thunder, and it is not from the clouds above but from the earth below!" The crow was frightfully agitated.

"And this thunder," said Sintus. "Is this thunder the sound of the earth shaking?"

"No, my King," said the crow. "It is the sound of many paws and the patter of tiny feet. My King, it is an army, and at its head is a great wolf."

Sintus immediately flew to a branch above and forgot the half-eaten mouse. *The wolf!* he thought. If there were a wolf coming this way with an army, it could mean only one thing: the wolf must be returning to claim what he considered to be his own—the field. Sintus felt the rush of coming destiny. If his band could join with the wolf, what power they would have! Sintus would claim his rightful place as King of the murder, with the wolf guardian of the wood and field. He called out, "You must away! We must welcome the wolf!"

Darus immediately flew to his side.

"But sire!" said Meeki. "This is no army to be greeting with open wings! They are an army that would eat a crow as soon as look upon them! There are coyotes in the number. And there are innumerable other snakes and lizards. And there is something else. Something dark and nearly as large as the wolf, a thing I do not know. The whole of them are coming with a mighty crashing as never heard before in this land! We must keep distance!"

Sintus glared at the scout. "You must be the one to let the wolf know of the prince's coming. You must greet the King and make him an offering."

"King!" called Meeki, finding a new fear. "And if I were to greet them, what gift could I give they could not take if they so chose?"

"As my gracious servant you will make an offering of the goldenrod flower."

Meeki gulped. "But, my king! If I were to do so, they would surely kill me!"

"Not at all," said Sintus. "It would prove our intention to the wolf of our honor and our desire to join him. Meeki, your task is of the utmost importance! To bring a King an offering of the fall flower is tradition's rule. There are many along the stream we passed just lately. Seek one out and take it to the wolf. He surely will not drink your blood with such an offering. The goldenrod means peace." Sintus gave a sly look.

"My King! Should we not go to them in force and circle above, calling our intention? Certainly we will be more effective as a group."

Sintus glowered at Meeki. "It is not for you to question my command. Go now before I take your query as treachery!"

Meeki shuffled. "Yes, my King," he stammered. And with that he was on wing and off upon his command.

When he had flown away Darus turned to Sintus. He was well learned in the flower offerings and their meanings. "My King, the goldenrod is certainly an offering of peace, but it is also an offering of blood. The blood of the carrier."

"Yes, my devoted general," said Sintus. "That is precisely my intention."

TORTRIX'S TAIL WAS wrapped lightly around Asmod's neck. Most of the snake's thick, scaly body was draped across the wolf's back. Normally, he kept his triangle of a head facing backward to the score of animals that followed Asmod's lead, training a careful eye on them all. He did not trust any of them. He had seen one of the other copperheads speaking to the king snakes and coyotes in hushed tones. He watched them with spiteful suspicion.

They had come but a short distance from the cliff they had called home, but already more animals had joined them, a family of foxes among them. They moved across the land in a wave of devastation. Each mouse den they came to they broke apart and killed all that hid within. When they came upon the nest of a grouse, they found her chicks hiding, frozen with fear. She must have been close. Perhaps she even watched as the coyotes ate each small bird. The head of each was presented to the wolf, and he gulped them down lustfully.

Tortrix heard it first: the caw of a single crow. It called out a continuous greeting. "My friend," said the copperhead to the wolf. "It would ssseem we have a visitor on approach."

"Ah," said Asmod. "I hear a crow, yes. An envoy from the field of home? Come to greet me?" He laughed. "Surely not."

They listened.

"Peace!" called the crow in approach.

Asmod and the others stopped and watched the approach of the bird.

"Peace! Peace to you and an offering!" cried Meeki as he landed awkwardly at what he hoped to be a safe distance from the wolf's jaws. Within his foot was clutched a golden flower. "I bring you greeting from Sintus, rightful heir to the throne of the Murder's Tree."

"Heir?" asked Asmod. "And why is he not yet crowned King?"

"He is near and will be coming shortly. I am but an envoy, a messenger," said Meeki. "I am commanded to come and to make this offering. Surely he will tell you himself of the treasonable usurpations at the field, only yesterday."

Asmod showed his teeth. "And what might this offering be?"

"I bring you the goldenrod flower! The sign of peace!" He carefully moved a bit closer to Asmod. Tortrix peeked out from behind the wolf's ear. Meeki saw the snake and started.

"And peace it shall be," said Asmod. "Now, come close with the flower. You must lay it at my feet as is tradition."

Meeki quivered as fear gripped his heart. He stood firm. "Yes, great wolf," he said, but remained standing in the same spot.

"Now," said Asmod quietly. "Do it now."

Meeki slowly moved before the wolf. And then, with as much courage as he could muster, he looked the great beast straight in the eye.

"Again I say: lay it at my feet. *Lay it at my feet and bow to me.*"

Meeki reached out his foot and set the flower down before the wolf. Then he bowed his head. With one swift motion Asmod opened his massive jaws and clasped them down around the crow's upper body, and with one bite he removed the bird's head, neck, and a portion of the torso. The wolf shook his head, and the remainder of the body flopped jerkily, and then lay still. One of the bobcats rushed in and grabbed it. Then Asmod began to chew hungrily, and after he had swallowed the crow he ate the goldenrod flower. The coyotes began to yelp and the foxes to bark. Not far away, Sintus and the rest of his band heard the animals calling.

"Meeki has made his offering," said Sintus. "Now let us go to the Wolf King."

Sintus and Darus flew in bravely and landed directly at the wolf's feet, the other crows flying into the trees above. And the prince told the wolf of his being cast out of the field, and he allotted his number to the wolf's aid, asking that the wolf join his quest likewise. The wolf smiled at the crow and did not eat him, not just yet.

Asmod told Sintus of his destiny to be the King of the wood and guardian of the field, promising to establish the prince crow as King of the Murder's Tree and that together they would rule, side by side. Sintus believed him. So the band of crows joined the army of predators and they moved on, together. And with them came the hell of destruction.

Chapter Eleven

A Whisper Within a Dream

Cotur Ada was standing in the field with the wind moving his feathers softly. He was not old anymore. He was as full of life and wisdom as he ever was. Beside him stood old King Crow, who likewise was young and strong, his stance proving authority and strength. They were face-to-face, their eyes set on each other.

"Your son must be King," said old King Crow to Cotur Ada.

"If my son is the King, numbers innumerable will die—not only my children but yours also," said Cotur Ada.

"This is the order. . ."

Then Cotur Ada lowered his head and began to cry.

Old King Crow sat down and closed his eyes.

There was a ripple across the scene, and when the birds looked up again, they were old and worn. And old King Crow flew, and when he did his feathers burst apart, going in every direction, a winged skeleton departing to the sky.

Cotur Ada leaned down to the ear of the young sleeping quail. Ysil heard the voice loudly within his ear. "Off with you, child," the bird said. "Up and off with you. See what you will today. Do not sleep the day away, for not far away the true heart's treachery of your brother quail is exposed. Up and off with you! Up and off with you! Up and off with you! Up and off wit—"

YSIL AWOKE WITH a start. It was truly his grandfather's voice that had awakened him, it had to be. He searched around for the source of it, for Cotur Ada. There was no way it could have been only a dream. But then he remembered the horrors of the afternoon on the previous day, and the memory covered him in a blanket of sadness. He felt hot tears rise to his eyes even as the words of Cotur Ada still echoed in his heart.

He looked about the thick brush where they slept and saw that the sun was barely halfway across the sky. After the encounter with the raccoons, they had moved on down the trail until they found a huckleberry thicket and decided to take a rest. He had not expected to sleep for long but had done so, as had his fellow journeyers. He saw three other forms sleeping near. Harlequin and Cormo lay still; only their soft intake of breath betrayed their camouflaged forms' existence. And there was Gomor, lying on his side in the warm sunlight as if merely resting, but Ysil knew him to be sound asleep. But where was Monroth? Where were the foxes? Then the words of his dream came back to him.

Up and off with you. See what you will today!

Ysil carefully moved out of the brush, making as little noise as possible, hoping not to awaken the others. He took to wing and flew to the tree above to get a better look around. From a good distance away he heard voices. He stealthily flew from one branch to the next, drawing closer so as to understand the voices.

"Well, you have stayed true to your word!" It was Puk. "What a nest you have shown us!"

"Yes," said Monroth. "But be quick in your feast lest the others wake and find us here. They would not understand my leading you to such as these."

Ysil heard a high shrill squeak and knew immediately what Monroth was doing. He had led the foxes to a den of mice. This was a dark thing for a quail to do, unheard of. Quail and other prey were bound together by like needs and common fear of predators. Monroth was breaking order. This was as great a sin as Ysil could think of. He wondered how Monroth had known of the den, then remembered his talk with Harlequin the day before. So Monroth *had* been this far. He must have traveled here often enough to learn where the mice nested.

Ysil felt the sting of Monroth's betrayal like the stab of a bodark thorn. He ducked his head and fell to the forest floor, barely fluttering his wings, fearful his flight could be heard by foxes' wary ears. He ran a bit back toward where the others slept before he took wing, flying as quietly as possible from tree to tree.

He settled to the ground and moved into the brush. Gomor was awake now, resting quietly. The others remained asleep.

"Where have you been?" asked Gomor. "Where are Monroth and the foxes?"

Ysil considered. He knew that if he were to tell of Monroth's betrayal they would be forced to go on without him and the foxes. How would Harlequin take it? Could they make away before Monroth and the foxes came back? He had to think quickly. "I need to wake Cormo and Harlequin before I tell what I have seen of the foxes and Monroth," said Ysil.

Many visions flashed through his head as he reached his wing to Harlequin's sleeping form. The voice of Cotur Ada seemed so real, so alive. But he had surely been dreaming. He checked his grandfather's feather within his breast. It was still there, carefully tucked away.

"Harlequin, Cormo, you must awake," said Ysil. "We must immediately away. I have dire news to tell."

And so, quickly, Ysil told the others of what he had seen, and Harlequin cried but said little. He had feared she would not believe. But she had not questioned him, only wept as the three quail took wing. And with the burden of the knowledge of their friend's betrayal heavy in their hearts, they flew in the direction of the rising sun, toward the river. They went fast down the trail, now staying within the branches above, forever looking back over their shoulders to check for pursuit. On the ground, Gomor the rabbit ran and did his best to keep up with the quail.

MONROTH WALKED WITH Drac and Puk through the thicket to the spot where they had left the others sleeping. When they reached the thicket, they found it empty.

Monroth stammered. This could mean only one thing: the others had found him out. He quivered, suddenly feeling more alone than ever before. He gave an awkward smile to the foxes.

Drac gaped back at Monroth. He showed his teeth. "Well, well," he said. "It seems it's only the three of us now."

At this Monroth trembled.

OPHREI SAT IN the midst of the tree and listened to the call of the geese. They were talking of the weather to the north, how there was a storm coming. The geese above were considering taking shelter early. They would take cover in cattails beside a pond or river and let the storm pass. Ophrei cursed the coming storm. But he felt that any storm of snow, rain, or wind was not the one to be concerned with. And though dark was still many hours away, he was sleepy and dazing. The sun was hot, and even though the day's warmth was not near its full, he felt within his bones the chill of winter as if the snow had already fallen.

The words and melody of the quail would not leave his mind. They played over and over in his head, and his heart was beating like a woodpecker's hammering beak.

At that moment a dove flew into the tree and settled down on the branch next to him. It fluttered to him and moved its beak nigh to the rook's ear. When he ceased his whisper, he flew away.

Ophrei sat and considered what the dove had told him and all it meant.

Nascus flew into the tree and landed next to Ophrei.

"Ophrei," said the prince, "shall I bring you some grain? Can I offer you any solace for this worry you wear upon your face?"

"The solace I seek will come with the sleep of death, my King in waiting," said Ophrei.

"Why do you speak in such dark tones? Surely the General has a plan in place for capturing and returning my brother?"

"The General's plans are in place, yes. And were these days as those before, I am certain that capturing the renegade would not be hard." Ophrei looked off and considered. "There is a storm coming, and the animals of the field may not make it back before its arrival. They may also encounter another storm . . ."

"Sage, you speak in riddles," said Nascus. "What is bothering you beyond the treachery of my brother?"

"My King, we must prepare," said the old rook with sudden resolve. "I will speak now a tale. Take from it what you may."

The rook closed his eyes and ruffled out his feathers. There was a gust of wind, and after that all fell deadly still.

"Once there was a small tree at the edge of a great, deep forest. And within the tree was a hollowed-out place. Within the hollow was a robin's nest. The old mother robin raised many chicks in the nest and took a great pleasure in it. She kept care of her children and grandchildren and loved them with a true heart. There came a day when the leaves were golden and the wind so still that she sat at the base of the tree and watched her babes playing and searching for worms and grubs. She was weakened and tired and fell to sleep below the branches. She dreamed that the earth gave up its bounty and worms were crawling out from everywhere. She and her brood harvested every worm that crawled out and filled their bellies. She slept on and on, her dream so sweet and full of bounty. While she slept, there came a migration of eagles and they descended upon her babes and took them all, not leaving one. She awoke to find herself alone. Within the nest was one last egg, but she had been so consumed with her other children she had not sat upon it. When she went to warm it she found the chick within dead. She sat in the tree all winter and did not eat. Come spring, a man cut down the tree and burned it. Her body and that of her dead chick he burned also."

Ophrei hopped down and pecked at his nest. He removed a strip of bark and replaced it with another. He flicked out a spiderweb and settled in.

Nascus ogled the old rook. "You speak of our tree, that a dark time is upon us. This I can gather from your tale. But who are the eagles? There are no eagles in this place."

"Nascus, we have been asleep for too long," said Ophrei. "We are fattened and the lesser animals abounding are fattened likewise. We have seen these days as a golden harvest, as our due reward in life. But we have not prepared for what must come. We have been but dreaming." He settled uncomfortably into his nest, his voice lowered to a whisper.

Nascus watched him thoughtfully.

"A day is upon us," he went on, "that few have dreaded. We have been too secure in our lives."

"What do you speak of?" asked Nascus. "What day are you meaning? Surely my brother and his forces can be defeated."

"Your brother, I am afraid, is but a small part of the evil," said the rook. "He is on his way back to us even now. If it were but he and his band, we would prepare for the battle and go to the task. But there is a much greater threat. Your brother now flies above an army much greater than any he could muster alone. I am afraid his small band is to be counted among one much greater. The doves have told me. The old quail was no fool. The wolf is returning."

Chapter Twelve

The True Order

DRAC, MONROTH, AND Puk set out after the quail, the birds' scent still fresh in the air. They went on for a distance. Then Drac stopped and turned to Monroth.

"Was this quest you were on with the others your own, quail?" he asked. "Was the old bird your grandfather?"

"No, he was not," said Monroth.

"Then why do we pursue the birds?" asked Drac. "Let us instead keep a pace away and wait on the trail for their return. Perhaps they have lost their trust in you, eh? Maybe one of them saw us a-feastin' on those mice you took us to, eh?"

So the fox had come to the same conclusion he had. "Yes, I suppose that must be why." And when he spoke his agreement aloud, he realized were it true, his life from now on would be forever changed. Once the others told the covey of his betrayal, he would be cast out. *Once they told the others . . .* Then the thought came to him: *What if Ysil,*

Cormo, and Harlequin never made it back to the field? What if he were to turn them over to the foxes and beg them kill them? The thought made him even colder inside. He could almost imagine doing such a thing to Ysil and Cormo. What benefit were they, anyway? But to Harlequin? She must surely hold some use to him still. And besides, he desired her as mate. If she had not been the one to observe his sedition, could he convince her that he was only protecting her by turning Ysil and Cormo over to the foxes? Possibly he could, yes. Then another thought occurred to Monroth: *What if the others never came back from their mission to the hawk?*

"Yes," said Monroth. "Let's stay on the trail and wait for their return." He needed time to think over his choices.

GOMOR PANTED AND ran, hopping fast to keep up with the quail in the trees above. *Why am I here?* he thought. Since the quail had fled the brush, leaving Monroth and the foxes behind, he had been asking himself this same question over and over. He knew that the journey they were on was dangerous, and since danger was all a rabbit knew anyway, at least this was normal. But why seek out more? Most rabbits' lives were short and ended painfully. He had always accepted this; still, he wanted to enjoy the life he had. He lived for his friends—that was true—and would protect them if needed. Still, this was not his fight. If the hawk were to return to the field, it could only mean the loss of numerous rabbits to its talons. Yet he understood the wisdom Cotur Ada had lent them and the importance of following his dying command. The command of a grandfather was always to be followed, even if death were sure from its following. He steadied his resolve and ran on, the quail high above looking down to him regularly to see if he was still below.

Ysil landed in a great maple and looked down to Gomor. "Let's rest for a bit," he called, then flew down beside his good-natured companion. "We should be far enough away now that we can at least slow. But we must stay ahead. I'm not certain that Monroth will pursue us, but he likely will. He may also take it as a chance to be done with this quest. Gomor, I believe his treachery is long-lived, past and future."

Harlequin and Cormo flew down. Ysil quieted. When Harlequin lit next to him, Gomor felt a rush of peace move through him.

She smiled at him. "Quite a run, Gomor. Never thought you would keep up."

"Me neither," said Ysil. "But we really had no choice. We don't know if Monroth and the foxes are just at our tail."

"It is a sad thing to be running from a friend, but the saddest thing I feel," said Harlequin, "is the realization that if he has betrayed the mice, he may betray us just as easily. He may have already done as much." She stared down to the dry earth at her feet.

Gomor knew she was sad. The place she had in her heart for Monroth was now empty. "Certainly he has not betrayed us," he said. "He has little regard for mice, but he would not betray his own kind."

"How can we be certain, Gomor?" asked Cormo. "In some ways, the mice *are* our kind."

Gomor was silent. Harlequin continued to look down.

"We can't be certain he has not," said Ysil.

They continued on at a quick pace but stayed on the ground. They followed the trail in the direction from where the sun rises. The day wore on and a cool wind came. With it, rolling clouds and a chill. They kept pace with the wind as best they could, at times flying, at times running. They were tired but kept going, the command of Cotur Ada driving them.

At three-quarter sun, they crested the top of a small rise and suddenly were astounded by the view of the Great River below. They had made a good distance in a short time. It meandered through the valley, snaking its way from one direction to another, then made a vast loop in its turnings, creating a great peninsula of land. They could see the trail going down through the trees and winding to the muddy edge of the water.

"The river," said Ysil. "I have heard speak of it all my life but never seen it."

"None of us have," said Cormo.

"None of our families have," said Harlequin.

"Perhaps Cotur Ada," said Ysil.

"Yes, perhaps," said Harlequin.

"But why?" asked Gomor. "It is so close."

Immediately, all eyes were upon him. With that stare, the answer came abruptly. "Oh," he said. "Oh, yes, of course."

They all looked at the river. "The hawk," he said.

IT WASN'T THAT the land about was without quail, rabbits, or other lesser animals; rather, it was just the opposite: there was a good number. But the animals here were of a different temperament and attitude than the animals of the field. These were the deep woods and the dangers were greater. Animals were much more careful here, and the few curious eyes they saw peeking from behind the brush or trees above did not venture out in investigation; and they did not slow to pursue any watchers. They had their purpose, and they went on.

They pressed on as the wind continued to blow, and to the direction from whence it came they saw that a great cloud darkened the sky.

"There is coming a storm," said Cormo.

"Yes, certainly," said Ysil. "But it is a great distance off. We should keep going. We cannot falter when our goal is this close."

No one answered him, but neither did anyone stop. Ahead was a rise, and at the top of the hill was a grove of pine trees. The trail down to the river must surely be beyond. They moved into the pines, eager to find the pinecones the trees promised. They were getting hungry. But the view between the tree trunks stopped their hunger. There beyond was a precipice and a great drop. The grove was at the top of a cliff, and at the bottom of the cliff was the river. They gazed out over the land beyond it. On the far bank was a dense wood. But it was not the view of the river that commanded their attention; it was what lay beyond it. Past the churning water and beyond the wood were many men's houses, some tall and some short. There were great towers with smoke rising from them. Beyond the hawk's realm was the realm of man.

Ysil felt a great chill within his heart. This was where he had been commanded to go, and he had followed Cotur Ada's direction. The dying words of his greatly loved grandfather were as law. But within him every ounce of his being told him he must turn back; he must return to his home and huddle beneath the brush and pray for the best. He thought of Harlequin and her broken heart, he thought of Gomor and his willingness to journey with them on a quest of which he was a part only in friendship. And he thought of the hawk, somewhere below. The hawk who could take their lives even before they delivered Cotur Ada's message.

Ysil looked around. All his friends' eyes were on him. He knew what they were thinking: they were as afraid as he was, but no one said a word. Ysil mindfully trudged down the trail without eating from a single pinecone. The others followed.

THE COURSE WOUND its way down the precipice through hollows and clefts until it flattened out along the banks of the river, and then into a small clearing. The clearing was still and quiet. It was too quiet, in fact. There were no sounds of birds, which was strange. There came the hum of one of man's loathsome beasts. The thought of what it could be made Ysil tremble. He had seen the man's machine cutting the field, its giant blades turning with terrible power. That creature had been noisy and angry, but the contraption he heard now must be much larger, for its growl remained vociferous, though, undeniably, far, far away. To make such a great noise, it must be a fearsome creature, for sure. And he could see what he took to be a fog billowing into the sky from the direction of the sound, and wondered why man would make a machine that would breathe fog to block the view of the sky.

They continued on, the sound of the river surrounding them until finally it was before them, a great tumult of driving force, wide and immense. They all turned and looked one to the other.

"Should we wait until almost dark to fly across the river?" asked Cormo.

"I feel we should go now," said Ysil. "The hawk is likely out hunting. Perhaps we should be near his nest when he returns."

Then all eyes went to Gomor. He could not fly. He could not swim.

"Well, I guess this is as far as I go," said Gomor. The relief was evident in his voice.

"I'll just wait in that brush over there until you come back," said the rabbit.

"I hate to leave you, friend, but I don't think we should wait," said Ysil. "We need to find his nest before he returns. Then we can sneak in and hide beneath. Even if he is already there, perhaps we can call up to him before he sees us. If we speak Cotur Ada's name, hopefully he will listen. We have to believe what Cotur Ada said. If we can't find his nest, at least we can find shelter there before the day wears on too far."

Harlequin turned to Gomor. "You know I will be missing you," she said.

The rabbit laid his long ears to the sides of his head and looked down, dragging his back foot through the dirt.

"I will gather some food," said Gomor, being as cheery as possible. "If you return before dark, we can all eat before sleep. That is my prayer, that you return before dark."

"It is my prayer that we return at all," said Cormo, staring blankly across the river.

With that they gave Gomor their good-byes and with a great flurry took off as one across the thick brown water.

Gomor watched his friends' flight and saw them descend into a raspberry thicket and disappear. It was as if they had never been there at all.

Immediately Gomor felt the chill of loneliness set in. He felt exposed and isolated. He looked around for the closest shelter in this strange place. He saw a stand of water dock, crowfoots, and forked rushes near the river. Glancing up and around to make sure the sky was clear of danger, he moved toward it. He remembered his promise to find food and wondered if there would be some there within the coppice, maybe even some morels or quillwort. There were also mosses that could be delicious. Then there was a sudden rush of wind, and Gomor, on instinct, darted toward the soggy undergrowth.

Beneath the raspberry bush the ground was wet. This was a place where the river seeped into the soil. The three quail landed in the muck with a splat. Then they saw the white shards all around them. At first Ysil thought they were sticks, bleached by the sun. Then he realized they were bones; the bones of rabbits, mice, moles, small birds—quail. He looked down at his body and to the faces and bodies of the other birds, all covered with mud.

Cormo laughed, not yet noticing the bones. "Well, if the hawk sees us now, he'll think we're little brown grouse, not quail."

With a quiver Ysil raised his eyes to the canopy above. High in the very tree above the raspberry bush was the form of a great nest. "The hawk's nest is right over us," he whispered fearfully. Cormo started, his eyes going white and wide.

The other two saw the nest and chilled. There was no

rustling within the nest, and Ysil felt for sure it was empty—for the time. They waited quietly for a while, and then set to cleaning the mud from their bodies. Beneath the bush they preened their feathers as best they could. Ysil removed Cotur Ada's feather and shook the caking earth from it. Then he returned it to his breast.

"Let's move down the bank of the river for a space," said Harlequin. "There seems to be a path there with a thicket beside it. Let's stay hidden in the thicket. And for the sake of all order, let's watch that nest closely."

"Yes, I agree," said Ysil.

They moved along the path, keeping within the dense foliage wherever they could, forever mindful of the trees overhead and listening carefully for the sound of wings. The woods here were even quieter than those across the river, if that was possible.

Then, suddenly, the sound they most dreaded filled their ears. They all huddled tightly together and pushed deeper into the bush. The steady beat of the wings grew with each moment. *Thump! Thump!! Thump!!!*

This is insane! thought Ysil. *How could we hope to talk to the hawk? It would kill us at first sight. We won't be able to get a word out before it rips us to pieces!*

Then the sound of the great wings filled their heads. The hawk was just above them, mere feet away. *This is it!* thought Ysil. *This is the end!* But then the hawk was past them and crossing the river. Ysil chanced a glance and saw that it was flying low over the water. *Perhaps he's looking for fish,* thought Ysil. Then, with a great beating of his wings, the hawk was up in the sky above. Ysil could see its head, its sharp, curved beak. Ysil had never seen anything like the bird, only heard it described in stories. It was far greater than he had ever imagined, but it was not horrible-looking. For a moment Ysil thought it beautiful, then shuddered. *A beautiful thing of death.* Until lately, he had never even considered seeing one in the flesh. Now he had searched the thing out. And there it was, a thing of nightmares; but at the same time, the goal of their search. How could he ever hope to find the courage to speak to such a creature? The birds huddled in fright.

"This journey is hopeless, Ysil!" said Cormo as quietly as he could. "Just before dark we must go back across the river and home."

Ysil watched the hawk in awe. The great bird was hovering, beating its wings steadily and looking below. Then, without warning, the bird made a great dive, tucking its wings behind, and disappeared from view.

The quail peeked out from their hiding place. Then they heard the pounding wings of the hawk once again, but this time his flight was a bit more labored, for within his claws was clutched a meager furry brown form. And Pitrin the hawk flew directly for them. The quail shivered and hid. Cowering within the brush, Cormo and Harlequin tucked their heads under their wings. Ysil could not look away.

With a great rush, the hawk landed very, very close. With one look Ysil confirmed what in his heart he already knew. It was Gomor the hawk clasped within its talons. The rabbit cried in pain. Within Ysil a great anger arose. Gomor was his friend and had come to be of help to him on his quest. Now the rabbit was to die because of his friendship, and Ysil would be to blame for his death. And as the rabbit screamed, the hawk tore its beak into Gomor's fur.

Ysil's fear was overtaken by his love for the rabbit and rage at the hawk, and with a jump he was through the air and on the path. He landed close to the hawk, dangerously close.

"Please!" cried Ysil. "Please do not kill my friend!"

Gomor cried out from his grasp. "Ysil! Go! Fly while you can!" he screamed, his blood gurgling in his throat.

The hawk's eyes, cold and without mirth or spite, settled upon Ysil. "You are foolish. If I were not holding the rabbit I would kill you also, quail. Listen to my food's words. Fly now, fast and far if you want to live." And Pitrin lowered his head to feed.

"No!" cried Ysil, stepping even closer. "I am the grand chick of Cotur Ada! I beg of you to stop! We have come with a message from him!"

Ysil then pulled the feather hidden within his breast and held it in his beak for the hawk to see. With that the hawk did stop, settling its deadly gaze upon Ysil. He looked at the quail, Gomor's blood on his beak. "Cotur Ada?" A look of recognition crossed the hawk's face, and Ysil felt a shimmer of hope. "Bring the feather to me," said the hawk.

Ysil stood still for a long moment, then with all his courage moved closer to the hawk. He lifted the feather up to the great bird. Gomor's blood was everywhere, and he could smell the hawk's feathers, full of death.

"Cotur Ada . . ." said Pitrin, his eyes now full of deep fury and wonder.

"Yes, Cotur Ada!" cried Ysil, stepping back cautiously. The hawk stared at him. "He is now dead! He gave his life so that others could live. And he commanded me to find you. To beg you to return to the field of your birth."

"He is dead?" asked the hawk. Then the immense bird shook in a convulsive disgust. "I will not claim to know Cotur Ada."

Ysil was astonished. "Are you not the hawk Pitrin, the son of Elera? I know your tale. Cotur Ada sang of you and your banishment in a plea to the crow Ophrei. But the old rook would not hear his plea! He killed him."

"I am Pitrin, son of Elera, but I am no child of a quail. Now go, so that I am not disturbed in my meal." Then again the hawk's vicious beak descended and tore into the rabbit's supple flesh, ripping the hide away. Gomor screamed.

"No!" cried Ysil. "I beg you, no!"

The hawk now glanced up from his prey with a blank, dull look. "It would be just as senseless for me to not eat this rabbit as for you to stop eating grain. Now go."

"But I am begging you to return! Cotur Ada is certain the wolf will come back!" said Ysil.

For a moment the hawk seemed to shiver, as if this knowledge would influence him. But then he spoke. "This is no concern of mine," said Pitrin. Then the hawk lowered his head to feast.

Ysil could not watch. He was overwhelmed with sadness. He flew back to Harlequin and Cormo, who had not moved as they watched in silence and fear.

When he was beside them, he said, "We must flee now, while he eats! Gomor is beyond our help!"

And with that they took to the sky. And the three birds flew with all the strength they had back across the river and up the cliff. They flew on and on, emitting cries torn and broken, their quest failed, their heads and bones sodden beneath the dull black pains of all-engulfing sadness.

* * *

AND PITRIN THE hawk finished the rabbit. As he did, he told Gomor that he was grateful for his life, for the food. With his dying words, though he fought and tried to get away, Gomor told him he understood. This was the order. Pitrin took no pleasure in the kill, only from the feeding. He ate every bit of flesh that he could take off the bones. And then he carried the carcass to the water and dropped it in for the fish to pick clean. He had fed well and was grateful. He thanked the earth for giving him his meal. And he said a prayer for the rabbit's soul, that it might again become one with the earth, and that within it would flourish and bring forth more life.

Pitrin went to his nest and settled. He tried to sleep, but though his stomach was full and his body satisfied, it was to no avail. For the quail's words were locked within his mind, and the sound of the wolf's howl rang in his ears.

Chapter Thirteen

What Cormo Heard

THE QUAIL FLEW on through the falling afternoon sun. The wind had picked up and it made the flight hard, but they went for a long time without resting. When they did stop it was only out of exhaustion. They settled under the shade of a green willow near a stream and grouped close, weeping.

"What could we have done?" asked Harlequin, the first to speak since they had taken flight. "How could we have saved him?"

Silence answered. There was nothing they could have done.

Harlequin moved away from Ysil and Cormo and pushed her head beneath her wing, crying loudly now. Ysil moved closer to her and for a moment only looked on, his own tears still wet on the feathers of his cheeks. Then he moved in closer to her and settled down beside her and, with a tender purpose, settled his wing around her. He did what he could to quell her mounting heartbreak.

Her crying only grew stronger. “This is all I can take!” she said. “It was a fool’s errand we undertook! We have accomplished nothing!”

Ysil spoke no reply, considering her words. Then Cormo came close to them and settled his wing around her also. The three quail huddled together in their loss and sadness, their bodies and hearts sapped of the youthful strength they had been brimming with mere hours before.

Harlequin continued to cry, stronger, it seemed, with each moan. “I had considered Monroth as mate!” she wailed. “He did hold such a strong place in my heart. Now that can never be!” Ysil shifted uneasily. “And Gomor was my life’s best friend. This pain is unbearable!”

They continued to hold her, neither Ysil nor Cormo saying anything, just continuing to wrap their wings about her. Her cries kept on, but after a while they turned to a soft weeping, and finally she became quiet, breathing softly.

The wind whistled around them, its voice telling of the approaching storm. And its song pressed them to move on. Each of them heard it, though at first they did not grant it the attention it requested. They nestled until their misery somewhat subsided. Then the song of the wind became a flurrying rush as it grew in strength until it was forcing past them, now seemingly unconcerned of their directive. They tried to walk a ways. The leaves were blowing everywhere and the temperature continued to drop.

Cormo was fantastically angry and sad at the same time. He moved on ahead of Harlequin and Ysil and set off down the trail. The other two stayed close together, but he needed the space to think. The wind blew harder still. Far away a boom of thunder sounded.

The hawk was a murderer, he cursed to himself, but as soon as the thought came to him he knew it was not true. *The hawk was not as the crows. He did not kill without reason. He killed for food.*

He kept up a fast walk. There was a fork in the path, and he took to the right, almost without thinking. He kept on, his head down, his mind racing. It was a good time before he turned to look back down the path. When he did, Ysil and Harlequin were nowhere to be seen. Had they been out of view when he made the turn? Had they taken the other path? He had taken the right turn out of instinct, sure it was the way they had come. Had he been wrong?

He flew up to the top of a sugar maple, its branches gnarly and overgrown, and looked back the way he had come. He saw them nowhere. Then he heard it, even above the roar of the wind. It was like the sound of a moving river but rustling and patting. There were growls and laughs—and hissing. His whole body shaking with fear, he raised his head to look.

There, down in the dale at the base of the hollow, was a split in the path, and below the split was a great band of animals. He saw coyotes, foxes, and the forms of snakes slithering past. There passed two bobcats and two possums. And there at the lead was the colossal form of a gray wolf. He shook his head and closed his eyes, certain at first that he must be suffering an illusion. But when he opened them again, the swath of animals was just as real as it had been the moment before, far too real.

Cormo's first instinct was to fly, but then he realized the animals' route would bring them near him, though not so near as to see him. So Cormo resolved to stay in the tree, its leaves twirling and flapping. He felt camouflaged. He prayed his sense of security was not false.

* * *

ASMOD HAD A full belly. Still, when he was offered a rabbit or a raccoon pup or even a vole or sparrow chick, he would eat it. The animals were always hunting as they moved down the path, and the bounty was great. Asmod knew this was his destiny, to spend the rest of his days full and never hungry. He was content in this, but there was always more, and he would take everything he could.

"My fellow King!" came a call from above. It was that rotten brat crow, Sintus. He landed beside the wolf as Asmod tried to quell his disgust. *Fellow King!* The thought was not only offensive but also absurd. However, none of these thoughts did the wolf betray.

"We are but a half day's journey to the field," squawked the crow. "Shall we stop for the night so that we be ready for the attack tomorrow?"

"No," said the wolf. "We move on. We will surround the field during the night. Then attack at first light."

Sintus huffed. "And what of the crows, Asmod? The crows will not move at night."

Asmod said nothing.

"Do not question—follow," came the quiet and loathsome voice from the copperhead around the wolf's neck.

"I'm not questioning anything," said the crow. "It is a fact. Crows do not have the eyesight to fly at night."

"Then you will walk," said the wolf.

Sintus considered. Then, "Yes, all right, we will walk." Sintus felt this would surely slow the army down, and that they would never reach the field before dawn.

They then passed a tall stand of trees at the top of a hollow. High within one of those trees, two unseen eyes watched and listened to what was said. The wind settled a bit in a lull.

"What of the quail, rabbits, moles, and mice?" asked Sintus. "They are certainly to be our subjects and, of course, your prey. But what of keeping their numbers? Shall we require them to pay tribute with eggs? This has been the way of the crow."

"The quail will not stand," said Asmod. "The quail will fatten our bellies and they will lose number. The rabbits will run and disperse, but the quail of the field will not relocate. We will take them all."

Sintus sighed. "Yes . . . Yes, I suppose you are right. Your kind will grow fat, then, for sure." He laughed. "And there will be much more for the crows to reap, with the lesser gone."

The wolf's band moved on, and high in the tree Cormo was frozen in horror. He had not heard everything that was said as the wolf and crow passed below, but he had heard enough. The strength of the wind grew again.

AS THE SUN continued its descent, Ysil and Harlequin walked on in silence. When Cormo gained speed and moved on neither of them really noticed, so lost in their thoughts were they. It was not until they reached the fork in the path that they realized their debacle. Which way had he gone?

"I feel certain that the way we came was the path on the left," said Harlequin.

"Yes," answered Ysil, "that is the way we came. But how can we be sure that Cormo remembered? He has never had to remember directions before. Should we wait here for a bit and see if he returns, looking for us? He can't be far down the path."

"We are lost now," said Harlequin. "Though we may be correct about the path to follow, we are all lost."

He did not answer, but he knew what she meant.

They waited there by the path as the sun inched across the sky with no further debate. Either Cormo would return, or they would nest in that spot for the night. Then they heard a rustle down the path and knew it to be an approaching quail. They watched expectantly as Cormo came into view. They saw the fear and shock on his face.

"A great wolf!" he said, catching back up to them. "Oh, for the love of my nest, Cotur Ada was right! The wolf is come! I saw he and his band just over the rise there. They are moving to the field." And he told them all he had seen and heard. They shivered at the thought of being so close to that many predators. Within Ysil an immense fear grew, a fear not only for the safety of their own lives but for the lives of their kind and their order.

"What do we do?" asked Cormo. "Do we go down the path and chance meeting them along it? Certainly this path we stand on intersects with the same on which they travel. We must try to make it to the field before they do. We must warn the crows of the wolf's alliance with Sintus."

Ysil cringed at the thought of the crows of the field. He had just seen them kill his grandfather. But he knew Cormo was right. If the order of the field was broken, all animals would suffer, perhaps numerous would perish. "Yes, to make it home before dark we must find another way," replied Ysil. He looked intently into the sky, then back the way they had been heading. "Let's go carefully beside the brush at the side of the trail. Perhaps we will find a hidden path. I need to get bearings on the field."

And so they went on quietly for a distance, and the wind was at their backs, for which they were grateful. They were afraid to take to the trees in fear the wolf's army would hear their flushing.

It was Harlequin that saw it, a small and nearly hidden path that shot off to the south. "This looks to be a path toward the field, I think," said Ysil. So they ducked through the small opening and followed the trail. As they went along, the grade grew steep and they climbed a hill. As they neared the top, they saw below them a stand of cedars. Then they heard the singing in the air, a whispered but joyful song. The voices, though soft, were large and deep. "The deer," breathed Cormo under his breath.

Foolish, foolish young and bold!
Careless, prancing fools . . .
Careful, careful, when we're old.
Now our numbers few!

Faster, faster, jump up quick!
Only feed at night.
Hope the boom of hunter's stick,
You elude in flight.

Antlers branched like sycamore,
And lover doe gives favor.
Crash and wrestle—rivals war,
Her bounty for our labors.

And if we were to gain a boon,
With winter drawing near,
'Twould be to die a friend to moon,
For God will shed no tear.

A careful laughter echoed from the cedar grove after the song ended. Then all at once the laughter died. The quail heard a few hushed whispers and then silence. Deer had the greatest sense of smell of any animal. Certainly, they had smelled the quail, but what if they had smelled something else? Why would the mighty deer have been startled by the mere scent of quail?

Then a young buck burst out of the grove and ran fast toward them. They scarcely had time to react before he was on them. "Quail!" he exclaimed. "Quail, why do you hold the scent of the hawk?"

In shock, it was Harlequin who spoke: "We have been to the land of Pitrin the hawk. It is certainly the mud from beneath his nest you smell."

"And the smell of rabbit's blood?" asked the deer.

"The blood is that of our friend," said Ysil. "The hawk slew him."

A flash of yellow crossed before Ysil's eyes. What could it have been? *Much too fast to be a leaf blowing in the wind. Perhaps only an illusion*, thought Ysil.

"What reason would you have to go to such a place, eh?"

Then Ysil told him of the death of the King and the Reckoning of the crows. The deer was of late informed; the dove had already carried this word to him, he explained. He showed little interest in their story.

"The last thing my grandfather commanded was that we go to Pitrin the hawk and beg his return to the field," said Ysil.

"Why would your grandfather command such a thing?" asked the deer.

"He knew that the wolf was to return," said Ysil.

"I have seen it with my own eyes!" said Cormo. "Not an hour's walk from here, where the path breaks. The wolf and his band are but a quail's flight away."

Immediately a doe burst from the nearby grove. She was enormous, her body toned and strong. She was a good deal larger than the young buck, the biggest living thing Ysil had ever seen.

"I am Oda," she said. "I am mother of this band. Now, birds, come to the grove and tell us the rest of your tale. I can hear in your voices you are tired and in need of rest. We also have food."

They followed her into the grove. It was thick and dark inside, and Ysil counted nineteen deer within. There were six large bucks, gray around the mouths and still, staring at the small birds. Oda led them through the thick trees to a small clearing concealed therein. In the very middle of the clearing was a giant white oak, laden with acorns. Beneath the tree sat a massive buck, bigger and with mightier antlers than any of the others within the grove.

"This is Illanis," said Oda. "He is the elder of the deer. I am first wife to him."

"Greetings, little birds," said Illanis, his eyes dark and certain. There was a small bird perched on his shoulder, a finch. "Your cousin here at my side is Flax. He has told me your tale. Not only such, but since you have spoken to

Oda, Flax has flown over the wolf's band and counted their number. This is a dire time, certainly."

Ysil considered the small bird and nodded. The bird only chirped in response. Finches were fast on wing, surpassed by only the hummingbirds.

"The wolf's return affects us all in this land," said Illanis. "Long have I feared and foreboded this time. I have known since he fled to the dark land that someday he would come back." The buck raised his chin. "And so, Pitrin the hawk, eh? I knew his mother, Elera. She died sadly."

"We held counsel with King Crow," said Oda, "the day after Elera died. The hawks and deer hold balance. Did you know that, little quail?"

"We know only what we are commanded and what we see," said Ysil. "We are quiet and look only to the grain for our needs, and to the wind, I suppose. The workings of greater order have never been our concern. We have tended to our own."

The old buck smiled. "As do we all, little bird. But alas, to understand, think on this: with no grain, there are no rabbits. With no rabbits, there are no hawks. And with no hawk over us, the wolf returns. And with nothing left but the wolf, soon he will starve also." Illanis shook his great head. "This I have long known. We have been foolish not to prepare.

"Oda, we must gather our wise in number and hold counsel with the turkeys," said the buck. At this all three quail gasped. The turkeys were no friend to the quail; they rooted out their nests and broke their eggs.

Oda's smiling eyes gathered upon the small birds. "I see you are concerned about your rivals, the turkeys?" she said. "You need not be so. The turkeys have their place, as do the quail. Tend to your field as they will their wooded domain. This invasion will reach farther into the forest than the trees surrounding your field. It affects us all."

"There is more to the contest between the turkeys and the quail than you know," said Illanis. "There is a tale I will tell you. It is a story of the turkeys, and certainly not the quail. A tale of three quail and a turkey chick caught within a man's net. But the man had died and the net was forgotten. The quail were small enough that they could break through the netting, but the turkey was larger and could not get free. When the quail freed themselves, they promised to tell the turkeys of the trapped one within. But instead they found a great stand of grain and forgot the turkey. And the quail grew fat, and the turkey died. And so any turkey to chance upon a quail's nest will scratch it out. Assuredly the rivalry between the quail and turkeys is old, but it is one founded simply. The quail are of the field, and the turkeys are of the wood. Tread within each other's regions and you are a challenger for the grain. It is that simple. But now we are to gather against a common foe, and the quail could never hope to hold ground against such an enemy. You need the turkeys to have a chance at survival. Find wisdom in this."

The three quail looked at the deer in still wonder.

"Now," said Oda, "eat. Night will be upon us soon. Come first light you must away. There is a path continues on from here that will lead to the Murder's Field. You must go quickly, for time is short. I fear the wolf's band will not stop for the night. We have no envoy to spare that could warn your kind of the coming attack. Surely the dove related the coming to the crows."

"But what of our families and the others of our kind?" asked Ysil. "They were cast out with the other lesser animals during the Reckoning, but surely they are back by now, unless they were held up somehow."

"We will be upon the field before you," said Oda. "We will save what we can. But now we must go to the turkeys. We must beg their alliance before they take roost."

The old buck whispered to the finch an unheard message and the tiny bird disappeared in a yellow flash. Quickly, the deer readied and gathered for command and all left the grove.

The quail broke apart some acorns and ate what they could stomach, being as sad as they were. Then they huddled together in the shade of the oak and watched the nightfall. The wind began whipping strong through the dried leaves, many of which broke free their clutch and blew to the ground. And dark settled and the three fell into a deep sleep, as only quail can do with such a storm coming.

Then came rushing in on quiet wings the great horned owl. He landed in the lower branches of the tree and gazed down upon the sleeping quail. He watched them sleep for a long time and considered many things, all he knew and what he guessed. Hidden in a perch high above, tiny Flax watched the owl, and wondered why he did not kill the quail. Then, just before the early light of dawn crept into the shadowed grove, the owl spread its wings and soared away as silently as he had entered.

Flax never slept.

In the fading light, with the wind whipping mightily through the chaos of branches above, Monroth and the foxes waited by the path. Then, rippling across the land came the steady rumble of what Monroth could not fathom. The wind's strength was growing steadily more uncomfortable, leaving Monroth feeling the need to take shelter. But the foxes had urged him to stay close and to keep watch from the lower branches of a tree.

"I hear something!" called down the quail. "I think it's animals moving down the trail, many kinds of animals. Sounds like many paws!"

Drac looked at Puk and grinned. "The time is here, I see. Just as the elder promised. So, they have come," said Puk.

Monroth heard the words but did not understand. "The time? What do you mean? Who is it coming?"

"It's the sound of our future you hear," said Drac. Puk was grinning ear to ear, and there was foamy spittle in the corners of his black mouth. "That noise you hear is like a spring's thunder announcing the approach of a new order, quailsie. What comes are the armies of our kind. And we must join. And unless you would choose to join us"—and with that Drac smiled at Puk, a dark and meaningful smile—"you may flee."

"What?" called Monroth. "Flee? Flee what?"

"Why, the wolf, of course," said Puk, who broke into a fitful laughter.

"W-w-wolf? What do you mean, wolf? There are no wolves left."

"Why, there is one, certainly," said Drac. "And he is returned. My father is Preto, and he remembers the time of the wolf. The elder Puk spoke of was he. Two days ago my father went into a trance. We brought him half a litter of mink pups, but alas, he would not eat. When he finally awoke, his eyes had gone blind. And he told us of the coming of the wolf and commanded that we seek out his army and join with them. You see, Monroth, when we found you birdsies and that fat rabbit, we saw the chance to bring the wolf a gift."

"A gift?" said Monroth. "What do you mean?"

Drac and Puk both smiled a vicious grin, all teeth.

Then the full weight of all Monroth had done fell upon him, and with fear cutting through him like an eagle talon, he took to furious wing, flying with all the strength he had from the approaching army and the sound of the foxes' laughter.

He flew on and on, up the trail, praying that he might find the path back to the field. But as he flew, darkness descended and he nested within a thick stand of moss thistle. And when he closed his eyes, he instantly fell into a fitful and dreamless sleep.

Cotur Mono was worried. He hoped they had left the vultures with plenty of time to make it back to the Murder's Field before dark. He and Sulari had not led the animals on the route passing the man's house, deciding that going near the dogs with this number of prey would not be advisable. When Sulari had made the journey before, he had done so in one day, dawn to dusk. And though they had left during the middle of the morning, he felt they would make it to the field before night fell. When they had made the journey the day before, they had reached Olffey Field with daylight to spare.

But halfway through the return journey, he began to suspect they would not make it home before dark. The old golden rat, Roe, had fallen behind, and though Cotur Mono wanted to let the confounded creature stay behind—maybe he would get lost!—he could not do so. He and Sulari had left the field with all the animals under their watch and there were too many missing now; he could not afford to lose another. So he stopped their forward progress and went back to speak to the old rat. He found Roe sitting by the side of the path, chewing something, as it always seemed he was, and looking up at the sky.

When he approached, the rat looked up at him with yellowed, sleepy eyes. "When were you born, bird?" asked Roe.

"'Twas seven seasons since my first memory," answered Cotur Mono. "But that is of little consequence now, rat. We must away. The band is waiting ahead, and you are slowing us down."

"I have heard a whisper, Mono," said the rat. "It is spoken softly on the wind. A call of the hungry. I do not know what it is, but there are many hungry close. There are also many feasting. I can hear the very chewing of their jaws."

"Certainly, it is the grinding of your own teeth. And if there is such a group, none else have had this intuition. I have not seen a dove since we left the vultures' field," said the old quail. "Surely if so many predators are near, one would have warned us."

"Maybe the doves are not here anymore," said the rat. "Maybe they have gone south. Perhaps they have more important tasks than carrying the news to us. Or it may be our messengers are dead, their messages dead with them."

Roe shuffled his feet and stood. "You know, I have come to a decision. I am old, as are you, and I am tired of never being heard and always being hungry. I am tired of always searching and never being full." He snorted and blew a wad of mucus from his furry nostrils. "I am going to turn around and head back the way we came. I am going back to Vulture Field. Keep Incanta company."

Cotur Mono raised his brow feathers. "Are you really considering it?" he asked. "I mean, you are not that old; what, six seasons?"

"A bit older. Alas, if truth be told, I am wondering what it is we are going back to," said Roe. "As I said: I have heard a whisper."

"I know nothing of this whisper of yours," said the quail. "Just the ramblings of an old rat who, like always, is thinking with his belly. Now set your head to logic. For a rat you are not that old, too young to give up and go to the vultures' field."

"Oh, I am not giving up. Just choosing what I feel is the better option." The rat spat.

"Well . . ." Cotur Mono began and then thought to himself: *This is not really losing one of the number. I know precisely where the rat is going.* "We will miss you," said the quail.

The old rat laughed, the golden fur of his belly trembling. "Oh, dear bird! Do not take me as a fool! No one will miss me." And he turned and waddled off.

So Cotur Mono went back to the band and told the hare of the rat's decision.

"Well, so be it," said Sulari. "I feel the company of the vultures will suit him."

And the group continued. Even then he hoped they would have time to reach the field before nightfall, if they hurried, but some of the mice got lost in a blackberry thicket. There were six little mice trapped, entangled in the twined branches. The mother had called out to the little ones as they had crawled within, searching out fruit, but young mice listen to nothing. She had cried and cried their names the entire time Rompus chewed them out of the bramble. When they were finally liberated from the thorns, they set off again. By now Sulari and Cotur Mono were resigned to the fact that they would have to spend the night in the woods. It was much too late now to reach the field and the safety of their home nests and dens before dark. This frightened the leader quail. The reason they had gone to Olffey Field in the first place was so the band would not have to spend the night in the forest unprotected.

Cotur Mono spoke to the badger and asked him to go on ahead, to find a place to camp. Rompus darted off down the trail, the rest of the animals trudging on.

The badger returned in no time with news of a tight stand of sassafras trees ahead. This was a blessing in various ways. It provided places to hide and food also. So the group went on to the coppice and fed. The chicks, pups, and mice all played about the brush; the old ones gathered and watched. As darkness fell, the birds bedded down and the mice made dens. The badger kept guard.

Quite unlike a quail, Cotur Mono could not sleep. So he sat up and talked to the badger. As night continued, the wind rose to a gale and rain pelted down. The two animals grew quiet and listened to the sounds of the storm, huddled within the relative safety of a wild rosemary bush. And there, behind the sound of the pattering of the raindrops and the rustle of the gold and red leaves, Cotur Mono did think he heard a whisper of words in the night's windsong. He looked at the badger in surprise. Had Rompus heard it, too? But the badger only glared off into the dark, certainly seeing much more than the bird. And after a while the rain stopped, though the wind continued. The sounds melted with the whisper, and the old quail finally closed his eyes and slept.

* * *

ROMPUS THE BADGER watched the shapes move in the trees, the shapes of the bushes blowing and the leaves flying. And he saw quite well, even with the moon behind the clouds, and often the clouds would clear briefly and the light was vastly brilliant, for the moon was a full round ball at this time, and it glowed brightly.

It was then that the moon moved out from behind a cloud and its light shone down upon the thicket. With the moon this intense he could see clearly as in day. Rompus noticed something moving from behind the brush, and this shape confused him. Perhaps it was a rabbit about its midnight feedings? But then he realized it was too large. And then with the shifting shadows, the vague form was gone.

The badger rose and moved to the edge of the thicket, looking carefully for more movement. He drew closer to the brush where he had seen the shape. The brush was blowing mightily in the wind, its branches thick and furious. Closer and closer he approached. Was it a skunk in the night, curious of the visitors? Could it be Roe returning? No, far too large. He peered far into the brush now; his face only inches from the green.

In a flash, a great form leaped out and was upon him. The last thing Rompus saw was a giant ring of teeth closing around his head. Then there was a great rush of crimson and the world was pain.

Chapter Fourteen

Reunions and Separations

"WAKE UP! WAKE up, foolish quail!"

Ysil jolted from his sleep. What was that voice? Was that his mother calling for him to rise? Was it Cotur Ada beckoning him? Then his mind came into awareness of dawn's feeble light. He felt a cold wind blowing his feathers, then the form of another bird close to him. He opened his eyes. It was Harlequin, and though the chill of the night was still surrounding, he felt comfortable warmth rising from deep inside. She lay still beside him, fast asleep.

"Aha! I see your eyes are open, but certainly there is no waking mind behind them. Perhaps it is love keeps you dreamy?" The voice was small and shrill, more of a chirp than a voice. Ysil looked around but at first could not find its source.

"Where. . ." he stammered, "where are the deer?"

"Do you forget Illanis's words?" said the small voice. "The deer have gone to the turkey roost, to ask the great birds to join them in battle. And no doubt through the night have been searching out the raccoons and skunks. Are you really as much a fool as I take you for?"

"Who is that talking?" asked Ysil.

Then with a slight flush the small finch landed right in front of him. "It's me, you buffoon!"

Harlequin rustled beside Ysil and stood up. "Well, good morning to you, little finch," she said with some irritation. "We have not overslept, certainly. The sun is not yet in the sky."

"Of all days to rise early, this is the one," said Flax.

Cormo was now also awake.

"What is all the yelling about?" he mumbled. "Do you want to attract the wolf?"

"There is no chance!" said the finch. "I have already been to the wolf's camp, just at first twilight. Not far, but not so close as to hear your yapping. But you must up! I have hard news! Your band of family and kind was attacked in the night! Many have scattered."

Ysil shook with shock. Cormo and Harlequin gasped.

"What of the quail?" asked Ysil. "Did you see any quail?"

"Nay, but I did see a lone gray hare moving down the trail at a slow pace. And also a small band of tiny mice, so I know not all were lost." The finch flew in an arc up and over the three, then in a flash was back where she had been only a second before. "Now we must away! Do your best to keep up with me!"

With that the tiny bird disappeared. The quail jumped to the wind, their minds still thick with the fog of sleep, and took off after the racing blur that was Flax.

*   *   *

WHERE WAS HIS burrow? The old gray hare knew it could not be far away. But he could not remember why he had left. Was he looking for food? Had he been alone? His head hurt and he stumbled. His vision blurring, he sat down. Then a bright red filled his sight, and he thought, *Maybe I'll take a little nap, and when I wake I will remember why I left my burrow. And what I was doing on the trail.*

"Yes, yes," he stammered. "That is what I will do. Sleep. And when I wake all will be back in order."

And the hare went to sleep, in the very middle of the trail, with the blood drying on his head and his memory blissfully erased.

"SULARI!" CRIED CORMO and swerved drastically to alter his flight.

Ysil saw the hare then, lying still on the trail. The quail landed beside him. Flax was already there.

"He is asleep," said the little finch. "Wake up, old hare! You old overgrown rabbit! Wake up! Your den is on fire!" The little finch jumped around the hare quickly, crying out with excited purpose.

Sulari began to stir. "Hmmm? Fire? Where?"

Ysil moved in close to the hare, knowing that his eyesight was not that good. "It's me, Grandfather Hare, Ysil."

The old gray hare smiled, focusing in on the face he knew well. "Ysil, my boy, you are back. We were so worried about you! I am so relieved that you're—" His face froze and the smile was replaced by a look of fear and horror.

"Oh, no!" cried Sulari. "Now I remember it all! The wolf! And his army! We were all attacked! I—I watched as—I watched as they died. I could not help. I watched as the wolf and coyotes and foxes and other monsters killed so many of the rabbits. And then an enormous fiend burst from the wood. I have never seen its kind before—not quite as big as the wolf, but oh, so horrible. And it killed Cotur Mono! I only ran!" Then he broke off in a fit of crying.

The birds' eyes were open in frightful shock. Harlequin moved in close to the old hare and put her wing around his neck. She said nothing, and cried herself. They sat there for a while close to the gray hare and tried to comfort him. But the anguish the quail felt was just as strong as the hare's.

Then a voice came from the wood. It was a voice all of them knew.

"I am glad I returned," it said, and out stepped Roe. Behind him trod a small group of animals, some seven mice and, in their wake, four rabbits. Then out from the brush stepped eight quail, among them Erdic and Anur. Harlequin flew to them with tears gathering on her feathered face. Her two young brothers took to her sides, one beneath each wing. Ysil saw Sylvil in the group of quail; she moved away from the others and close to Cormo. She looked him in the eyes and some unspoken communication passed between them. She lay at his feet and he sat down beside her and patted her with his wing. There was blood on her shoulder and a cut in her neck. He moved close to her and nestled his head to her side. She smiled at him. "I am glad to see you, Cormo," she said.

It was then they all heard the sounds of crows approaching, cawing madly, immediately followed by the howling of coyotes and beasts. It was a chaos of sound that pierced their very hearts with all life's history of fear and flight. Ysil could liken it only to that of the man's machine, it was so deafening and maddening. All of them burst for cover and hid. And some flew farther but some found cover closer to the trail. Ysil flew away in a speedy fury and settled in the thorny branches of an Osage orange tree. He was alone, and the fear of the coming army pounded in his chest.

Flax flew straight up. He flew higher and higher until all below was small and quiet. And up in the heights, not far below the billowing, rolling clouds, he hovered in one place and watched. He saw the crows at the head of the army, flying in standard rank. Behind them were the forms of many vociferous animals, howling, yelping, seething, and noisome: the army of the wolf marching to war. And farther up the trail, past where the animals were hidden, he could see the Murder's Field. Within the field there were many crows, the Murder's Tree black with their number, their black bodies speckling the ground. Then it came clear to the finch, for he knew that there were far more crows in the field now than ever before. And also in the field and in the trees surrounding he could see the gray bodies of many smaller birds.

So that's what they have been up to, he thought. *The doves have rumored up an army of crows.*

OPHREI WAS BUSY within the nest of the King. He hopped and fluttered about, pulling out old snakes' skins, many of which disintegrated into a pale powder. There also were not a few mouse skulls and the occasional mole corpse, which had gone rancid through the summer heat. In the last month of the King's life he had not left his nest, and in his death spot there were still the stains of his bile and feces. Ophrei had waited too long to clean the nest, but now he must. The new King must have a fresh foundation on which to build. He picked through the parts that were of newer construction, this past spring's willow boughs and oak branches. Beneath, some of the nest was exceedingly old. Upon these branches rested the nest of the murder's King, as it had been and always would be. A lower portion was constructed from the limbs of an old chestnut tree, wormy and gnarled. Ophrei knew that there were no more chestnuts alive. The trees had been killed out by an angry wind long before his time. The nest was very old indeed.

But when the new King was crowned, he would put his own touches on it. So the old rook prepared the nesting area. This would be the day of the crowning. He knew it to be true. The wind had told him so.

And so Ophrei picked the white matter and black feathers from the nest and let them fall to the ground below. He was so consumed in his work that he had nearly forgotten that upon the field below was the greatest gathering of crows in this area in many years. Only in Miscwa Tabik-kizi were there such gatherings.

Two doves flew up beside the rook and watched him working in silence. After a few good minutes ignoring their presence, the rook settled his eyes on them.

"Well?" he said. "What news do you have for me today?"

But the doves did not answer, and he went back to his work.

After a few minutes of watching, the doves flew away.

But the rook knew what their news was, and likewise they knew they did not have to whisper it. The wolf was near. Dangerously near, now. And with him was the rogue prince.

Ophrei redoubled his efforts. *Not much time now to ready the nest for the new King.*

NASCUS WATCHED THE crows around the field with apprehension. The sound of their squawking and cawing was nearly deafening. The number was great now, and there were more arriving. Most of the birds he had never seen. The doves flew between the crows, whispering in the ears of many, relating things to them. There was a rogue prince en route to this field, and that alone was enough to gather a small army of one type or another. However, it was the return of the wolf that had built the legion before him. If a wolf were to take over this field, there might be one to take over their home fields. They were ready to fight, as most crows usually were at any given time.

The season of the raising of the Widjigo was approaching, and many crows were moving into the face of the cold wind already. None alive remembered the first calling, but the rooks told of its beginnings. The tale was passed down and down. Ophrei had told it to the princes when the three were but chicks.

The thought of the tale came to Nascus now and he shivered. As he remembered it:

Once, the birds and animals had been the only inhabitants of the land. There was stillness across the fields and waters, unbroken by the sound of man's machines, their work sounds, and their strange words. The animals had lived in peace then, and all order was as one. But man had come and brought great change. He had taken over the fields and carried death in with him. He had killed off many animals and held no reverence for the order of the kinds. It was then that the crows had established their order. It was at this time that the First Atonement was held in far-off Miscwa Tabikkizi, which was then only an open field with an oak grove in its middle. The crows had met to list their grievances with men, and many wished to find a way to get rid of them.

And so the crows had held council with the Wind, and the Wind had told them that man would never be driven out, that man was to stay. The Wind also told the council that should they ever hope to have influence in the world of men, they must continue to hold council every year.

But one crow would not hear the Wind and insisted that man could be driven out. So the crow, whose name was Widjigo, had begged the Wind to take him in and to feed him in breath to man. The Wind had finally allowed Widjigo in and had consumed him. But when the Wind had fed him to the men, the men had only blown him out. So Widjigo had become saddened and taken to the quiet places, where men never did go.

But then one man had taken his family to the wild parts, to where Widjigo was dwelling, and made his home there. And one night, while the family slept, Widjigo settled into the man's chest. And in his dreams, Widjigo whispered to him, deep into his hunger. When the man woke, he was enormously hungry. Madness overtook him, as if starving, and he went into the room of his wife and two children and slaughtered them like animals and ate them. It was in this way Widjigo the crow turned its anger into man's insanity and hunger for his own.

And Widjigo stayed in the wild places and spoke to the lonely and the lost, and some took on its anger and hungered for their own and ate.

But the council knew Widjigo would not drive man out. Though they meet still, every year, near a great burial site for men, which was once only the clearing with the oak grove. They hold a council with the Wind, so that men should be driven out of the world.

It was only there, at Miscwa Tabik-kizi for the Atonement, that so many crows gathered in one place at the same time. Now the gathering in the field below was rivaling that number.

And Nascus knew that the birds gathered here looked to him to lead them, that they were all here to strengthen the field's army and to fight the approaching danger. They were also here to further ensure that the King would be chosen today, that the darkness would be overcome and the new leader crowned. The army around him was gathered to help him fight this evil. He felt a brave pride rise inside. At the same time, he felt the coldest fear he had ever felt, for he knew that the number of crows and doves, though many, would never equal the strength of the wolf's army.

Ophrei flew down to him and settled at his side.

"The new King will be crowned today," he said. "This I know to be the truth." The old rook seemed at ease. Certainly, this somewhat calmed Nascus's heart.

"Rook," asked Nascus, "is this King to be me?"

The rook jumped. "Certainly it will be you," he exclaimed. "Of who else could the wind be speaking?"

"My brother, perhaps. Or . . ."

The rook wobbled and a wind shifted his feathers. "The wind would not tell me such a thing if it were not to be you," said the old rook. "This is surely true." He seemed resolved.

But Nascus was uneasy, and for some reason he could not get Widjigo's hatred of men out of his head. He feared that the army coming now was in many ways like man—certain, prideful, and purposeful to its own cause. He wondered if the wind had always known Widjigo's cause to be futile, and if, when it had taken the crow into itself, it knew of the madness it would bring. As the thought came to him, it tugged at his insides, conceiving another question: Was the wind to be trusted?

TORTRIX PEERED AROUND Asmod's great bulk of a head with the cooling breeze in his face. It would not be long until he took his winter's sleep. He must eat again soon. He was losing energy. Although copperheads needn't eat often, he had not fed since they left their home cave. In fact, he had scarcely left Asmod's neck. He watched the other animals and snakes feast on all they chanced upon, from the voles to the fully grown squirrels; the food was everywhere. A few had gorged and were paying dearly, their bodies swollen and cumbersome; they had been left behind. Tortrix had not wanted to be in the least bit encumbered by having his belly full, for a full snake was a lazy snake, and he must be forever watchful of the predators around him. Though they all were professing their loyalty to Asmod, Tortrix knew that they would, any of them, turn on the great wolf if they felt they would gain for themselves. He watched them always, forever on guard. But he could not go into the battle without something to eat. He had just not chanced upon the right-size meal. Too big and he would be slowed down, too little and he would not get enough energy from the food to ensure his readiness for battle.

Asmod whispered under his breath to the snake. His loyal friend did so only occasionally, as it was scarcely needed for them to talk at all. They communicated without speaking.

"There are more than a few quail and mice in the bush ahead," whispered Asmod. "I can smell them. I need not eat again before battle. I know you are hungry. I will stop and let you go on ahead. Go to the brush on the trail's edge and take the small bird within."

Tortrix's tongue slithered out of his mouth and took the wind in, and yes, he did smell the animals ahead. A good few of them. "Thank you, my friend," he said to Asmod and dropped his slithery body to the ground.

When Asmod stopped, the animals behind him halted also, each of them watching his every move. The crows above flew back a bit and landed behind the wolf. Sintus approached him.

"The snake will feed now. When he finishes, we move on," said Asmod.

"We are nearly at the field," complained Sintus. "We are within earshot. We dare not pause for long. The birds are quiet. Surely they know we are about to attack. They will be perched all about the field. Perhaps they will give it up without a fight. They could never hope to stand against such an army."

Asmod smiled. "Alas, I do feel we will have something of a fight in taking it over. I can feel the rise of hot blood in my ears. Always does my blood heat before combat."

Sintus huffed. "Yes, I admit you are correct. But any war is acceptable to take the field as our own. As long as it is my brother's blood you smell."

"Certainly it is," said Asmod. And the great wolf did not speak another word, just turned and sat down upon his haunches. The birds and animals watched the two prospective Kings, each one with their own questions, but none spoke.

Tortrix slithered on. He smelled bird, certainly a nice, plump quail. A fine meal. He moved silently through the foliage along the edge of the trail. As he neared the brush, he saw the shade of the bird's feathers almost perfectly blended with the browns, reds, and yellows of the brush and leaves. Tortrix tasted fear on his tongue. It was its fear that gave the prey away—it was always that way. The delicious little thing trembled, its meager breath raising and lowering its form spastically.

The snake crept close. His hunger grew as he prepared to strike. Within his head, the poison pressed down from overfilling sacs into his fangs, which began to seep with anticipation.

HARLEQUIN HAD JUMPED when the other quail did but had not flown far. She had been so startled that she had made it only to the edge of the trail. There was a thick brush there that looked concealing at the time. It was only when she had settled into the thick leaves that she had realized her mistake. She was too close to the trail. But as soon as she perceived her error, she heard the footsteps of the approaching army. If she flushed now, she would undoubtedly be seen. And if she flew, perhaps the other quail and mice would run or fly. They might all be killed.

And so she did not move, her head beneath her wing.

And then the approaching animals stopped. She heard the sound of their paws cease and the settling of the crows. She had not chanced a look. There was the din of a deep voice, dark and certain, followed by another, whispering slight and breathy. Then the sound of a crow, a voice she had heard before, that of one of the princes. The rest of the animals were quiet. But for her fearful breathing, she sat still as death.

Then things happened very quickly.

Chapter Fifteen

Ysil's Flight

When the quail and the rabbits and the rest of the band heard the coming of the predators, Ysil reacted on instinct. He had taken to the air first, his wings aflutter. All around him animals had run and the quail had scattered. He had been beside Harlequin when they were standing on the ground, but now she was not with him. Within the shelter of the Osage orange, Ysil quavered in anticipation. Where had she flown? He tried to remember. Had she taken refuge in another bush? He did not think so. Someone had flown near him, but he was certain it was Erdic, her brother. He struggled to remember. Then he closed his eyes and focused on the moment of chaos. Some of the birds had merely flown a short distance, and he prayed she had not been one of them.

But she had not flown far. He was sure.

He must go to her! He must find her. But how? There were so many predators around, and with the first flight of a quail, all might fly. It was their way. He closed his eyes tighter and listened to the wind. It blew its whistling tones, a chaos of many melodies. It offered no suggestions.

"Oh, Cotur Ada," he said out loud. "But that you were here to guide me!"

"I am always with you," came the voice of his grandfather from just next to him.

Startled, Ysil opened his eyes to look. There was no one there. He chilled. It was his grandfather's voice, certainly. But he was alone in the bush. Then he felt the brush of wings next to his and the flush of a movement. He looked, but there was still no one there.

Then, softly but with great urging, his grandfather spoke to him again: "You must away. She will fly, this is for sure, and when she does, you must be there to meet her. You must meet her in the air. Guide her to the bush where you were born. There you will be safe, for a while."

Ysil took heed. He closed his eyes for but a moment more, then opened them with fresh resolve.

"Yes, Grandfather, I will," he said, though there was not another living bird near. "Be with me." And he took to flight, back toward the trail, back toward the killers. He did so on faith in his grandfather's word, for he most certainly did not have faith in his own strength.

And as he breached the top of the trees, he heard Cotur Ada's voice once again, as if he were at the tip of his wing. "As I said, I am always with you . . ."

TORTRIX STRUCK, HIS fangs forced outward, his eyes black with lust. But even as he did so, something forced itself beneath his throat. It was a wing, the wing of a small bird. The snake was knocked off his striking and missed his target.

"Cursssesss!" hissed the snake.

"Fly!" said a desperate voice. "Harlequin, fly!"

Harlequin sensed a quick movement and upon instinct pushed off to fly, but she was moving too slow. She saw the snake striking at her. When she looked at the attacking monster, she saw its mouth wide, its fangs rushing toward her face. Then, with a flurry, something flew in the very path of its bite. A flash of gray and a rush of wings, and the snake was forced off mark.

Then came a familiar voice, a voice she had known since she was a chick telling her to fly. So finally she flew, her wings pushing the cool dry air beneath them. It was then she realized whose voice had commanded her.

"Monroth!" she cried.

She looked back and saw him take to wing also, flying low at the edge of the trail. Too low. Just before she passed out of sight, she saw a red furry form burst from the bush upon Monroth, taking him back down to the cursed ground.

Suddenly there were two quail flying beside her, one young and one old. But when she looked again, there was only one remaining: Ysil.

"With me!" he cried. "With me to safety!"

She followed him as he flew back across the trail toward the place of their birth.

Puk held Monroth in his mouth, the little bird fighting forcefully to free itself. The more it fought, the tighter Puk clenched his jaws. He looked triumphantly back down the trail, his head held high. The predators did not disguise their happy surprise. Even the wolf was staring with his mouth wide, his tongue dangling, and dark amusement in his eyes. But it was the copperhead who appeared to be enjoying this the most.

Drac stepped from the bush beside Puk. He smiled triumphantly to the snake and wolf.

"Not to worry," said Drac. "My friend here has retrieved you a fine dinner, Sir Snake."

Puk broke Monroth's wings and took him to Tortrix, and after eating him, the snake was satisfied but not too full. The wolf watched all this and took the moment to rest and prepare for the battle that was sure to come. So it was that Drac and Puk came into the favor of the copperhead, and likewise into that of Asmod the Great.

YSIL AND HARLEQUIN flew down into the familiar protection of the bush they had always known as home. But when they grew still, they heard rustling and whispers. They were not alone. There were three other quail in the bush. One of them was Anur, Harlequin's brother. When she saw him she flew down next to him and began to cry. Ysil came close.

"Monroth saved my life!" she cried. "Now he is surely dead."

"He loved you dearly," said Ysil, the tears coming to his eyes also. "Certainly he is redeemed. And there is the chance he escaped." He said this in hope. But even as he said the words, he knew that certainly Monroth was dead. He, like Harlequin, had seen the treacherous fox take their friend from the same air on which they had flown only moments before.

"I pray so also," said Harlequin, "but alas, I do not believe it. The fox has taken him, and he has delivered him to the snake in my place."

Ysil did not answer. He only moved next to Harlequin and nestled. Quiet settled around the bush, but for the breeze rustling the foliage. The wind was subdued now, as if it was saving its strength for the coming hours. Harlequin nuzzled up beside Ysil and cried. She laid her head upon his wing and pressed it beneath his throat and rubbed her neck up to his.

No other quail had ever done this to Ysil, and he felt a flush of warmth within. It was then she came full into his heart. He nuzzled comfortably back. And still she cried. And behind her Ysil saw that Anur had gone to sleep. And so he and Harlequin moved together in the way of the quail, and comforted each other gently. Ysil cried along with Harlequin, and within a few minutes she fell asleep, their heads resting on each other's wings. It was mid-morning, and as Ysil likewise passed through the veil of consciousness and joined her in a brief exhausted sleep, he saw his grandfather's face. And his grandfather was crying also.

Ysil awoke with the sound of crows' screams beating his ears. Harlequin remained sleeping, her brother near. *The battle! It has begun!* But no sooner had this thought crossed his mind than he realized his error. This was not the sound of battle. This was the screaming of anger, but no battle, not yet. He was confused.

Ysil whispered softly to Harlequin until she awoke. Her red and worn eyes opened feebly and stared directly into his.

"What is that screaming?" she asked.

"I have the feeling that the wolf has made it to the field," said Ysil.

"Ysil, let's just go," she said. "Let's leave here and never return. You and I—right now." The skin around her beak was puffy and her voice was haggard.

"I know," he answered. "I want to leave here also." Ysil looked off, seeming to see through the brush to the field beyond.

"But we can't, can we?" asked Harlequin. "I mean, there have been too many die for us to leave here and give up. We must go to the edge of the field, mustn't we? We must bear witness." She breathed in deeply, summoning all the strength and courage she could find. "And we must hope for a way to help free the field from the rule of the wolf."

Ysil was quiet for a moment, still looking through the thicket and toward the pandemonium beyond. "Yes, we must watch. And though I cannot fathom what it may be, we must hope for a way to help," he finally said.

She rose and moved with him out of the nest and through the copse, as silently as they could, until they came to the edge of the field. And there within the boscage, still and quiet, they saw the hidden form of another quail. As they neared they realized it was Cormo, who looked up at them with wide, fearful eyes. They settled down next to him.

In the field there were the shapes of many animals, and at their center stood a great wolf. Tightly wrapped around his neck was a bright copper-colored snake, content and bloated. All around the wolf and snake were coyotes, foxes, weasels, minks, and not a few black rats. About their feet moved the slithering forms of snakes, along with quick skinks and other lizards. Within this number, close to Asmod at that, were the treacherous Drac and Puk. Ysil trembled in anger. There were other animals, some that Ysil could not identify. Scattered among them were the rogue crows: Sintus and his flock. Most of these animals were quiet, though some called defiantly upward.

The chaotic din that had woken Ysil did not come from the intruders, who seemed completely surrounded, though confident. They had moved into the field unchallenged by action. Instead, a vocal challenge was issuing from the trees around the field and also from the Murder's Tree, which were all covered with more crows than Ysil had ever seen in one place. The golden and red leafed trees were nearly black with the forms of the birds. And among them were an abundance of doves.

Out of the Murder's Tree flew a lone crow, screeching and crying. It was Jackdaw. Jackdaw the messenger, Jackdaw the jester, and on at least this one occasion, Jackdaw the brave.

"Woe to you!" cried Jackdaw. "Woe to you all, intruders!"

He settled into the midst of the predators. "I am come under command of the great and wise General Fragit, who speaks for the heir to the throne! You are all to leave now! Leave this field at once or be killed, every one of you! Except Sintus—you are commanded to stay and continue process in the Reckoning!"

The wolf laughed. "And it would be this army of birds that will stop us? We are here to take this field and today will do so. We are also here to supplant your chosen king. We do not recognize your Reckoning. You would be wise to join our number now, messenger."

Sintus was at Asmod's side. "Jackdaw, you may fly back to the Murder's Tree and tell the General that his challenge has been answered, that he may flee and perhaps bargain should he wish, but that we are taking the field."

Jackdaw fluttered into the air and back down again, shaking his head and cawing. "I will tell him you are a fool," he said and turned to take wing. The copperhead came down off Asmod's neck and, just as Jackdaw flew, the wolf leaped upon him and took him from the air with his teeth. He brought the screaming crow to the ground.

"I am the messenger!" said Jackdaw in great pain, the wolf pushing him down with mighty paws. "You cannot kill me."

"Well," snarled Asmod, "let your death be my answer!" And he brought his teeth together around the bird's body, tearing him in two with one great bite.

It was with this action that the war of the Murder's Field began. As the wolf bit down, a great cry came up from the trees surrounding and an even greater one from the Murder's Tree itself. And all at once the crows burst upon wing. They descended in cawing fury, their beaks and talons sharp. Below, every animal and reptile raised its head and opened its mouth in an eager, rapturous scream. And the teeth, claws, and fangs were the greater number.

Chapter Sixteen

The War for the Field

FLAX WATCHED. THIS was always what he did; he never acted unless he first considered every possible happening, and only then if he felt certain of the outcome. When the wolf leaped upon the messenger crow, he knew he had seen enough. Fast he flew, as fast as his wings could carry him. He was a flash of yellow through the high sky, and no one saw him. He flew fast and with an understood purpose. The battle had begun. He flew with the speed of a great wind to the turkeys' roost. As he descended, he saw that the deer were still holding council with the turkeys. He landed upon Oda's upper neck, just behind her ear. She did not react as he landed, not even as much as to turn an ear in the tiny bird's direction.

She was speaking. "But you must know," she went on, "even if it were an army of weasels, your future would be in danger. They would search out your eggs and eat them all, every last one. But this is not only weasels, this is coyotes and foxes. And a great wolf at their lead. You must join in our battle."

"What do we gain from such?" asked Butry, the leader of the turkeys, the King Tom. When the deer arrived the night before, the turkeys had made an early roost and would not come down. So the deer had searched the nearby forest and warned any possums and raccoons not already aware of the danger of the wolf and his army. Then they had bedded down beneath the turkey roost and sheltered from the storm, preparing for the possible battle to come. It was not until just lately that the birds had descended and heard the deer's plea. "We will not fight. We will wait. Should the predators take over, we will leave this area. We hold no heart to this roost."

"But how can you not see?" asked Illanis. "You may sit here and wait, but if you do, they will come upon you in the night, as you sleep. No matter where you may roost on high, they will come upon your young who do not yet fly and take them from these ground nests you guard. Should you try to defend against their midnight attack, you will all die."

"We will not fight. We will wait." Butry was resolved.

Oda sighed. It was then that Flax whispered into her ear the news he had.

"The war has begun," said the finch.

"Damn you, you stinky, foul turkeys!" she said. She looked at Illanis and a silent communication passed between them. He snorted in agitation. And the deer took to hoof, the small finch flying with them, and they raced through the woods as fast as the finch had moved through the high sky. As they went, there were shadows that joined them and instantly sped to their pace. Flax heard the beat of hooves and the rhythm of many breaths around and knew that with each step more deer joined the charge. And as he flew with the deer, there joined them small scurrying shapes from the trees, all running and jumping from one tree to another. Squirrels. The deer ran on, their great legs driving their purpose.

NASCUS FLEW CLOSE behind the General. When the wolf had attacked Jackdaw, the General screamed, "Into battle!" and flew with a raging fury straight toward the wolf. His battle cry was not needed to move Nascus, or the rest of the crows for that matter. They took to air as one.

Nascus's wings beat double his heart's time. He felt the heat of fear and of certain bloodshed. Then he saw his brother take wing and fly straight toward him. Sintus was always the greater of the two, older and stronger, and more headstrong and prideful. Already there were crows upon the coyotes and foxes, which were jumping up with raised fang and tooth to meet the birds' descent. One crow jabbed its beak into a gray fox's eye, and the beast howled in agony. It thrashed upon the field. Then the same crow that had taken the fox's eye was bitten from behind at the nape of the neck by a coyote. The bird struggled to free itself from the animal's bite, but the coyote only shook its head in fury, the crow's feathers flying into the wind. Crows were taking the smaller lizards and snakes in their feet and flying them high into the sky and dropping them, so there was a rain of reptiles falling all around. Some would die upon impact; others, only stunned, would either be picked up for a second dropping or return to the fray. Snakes were springing their bodies into the air and biting at the descending crows in wrath.

The General was barely before Nascus now, bearing down on the wolf, who already had two crows lying dead at his feet. There was a third in his jaws now, bleeding and screaming. The crow did not have a chance, but still it thrashed about and pecked at the wolf's cheek and neck. The wolf seemed not to notice the large crow, almost to his left side. He remembered the wolf's missing eye, the one taken by Elera, and Nascus had a flash of realization. Fragit was attacking from the wolf's blind side. The prince felt a brief charge of hope. *Could it all really end this quickly?* If the General blinded the wolf, the others would fall away, or at least be dispersed with no leader to fear or command. He also knew just as well that if he or the General or both were killed, this murder gathered here to protect the field would likewise scatter—or join with the victor. The wolf shook his head, and the feathers from the crow in its mouth flew, blood showering through the air.

Fragit was upon him now, his beak readied for strike. Then through the air like a straight red stick came the bolting form of a great snake. The General was quick, but the snake was much quicker. Tortrix bit Fragit in the neck and brought him to the ground, the two thrashing in a vicious struggle.

Then Banka was at the wolf's ears, pecking and aiming for the wolf's lone eye. Asmod made one quick snap with his horrible jaws and grabbed the General's first in command. Banka's head went flying through the air and landed with a smack on the already bloody field.

Now Nascus himself was upon the wolf, his heart resolved to fight to the death. Then without warning something crashed down upon him from above. His brother Sintus! He had been occupied with Fragit's attack and had lost track of his brother. The other prince had taken to the heights and attacked from above. And as Sintus wrestled Nascus to the ground, the younger prince realized his mistake, perhaps the last one he would ever make.

Sintus pecked at his brother's eyes and neck, drawing blood. "You fool!" cried the crazed rogue crow. "You will die today! Die knowing I am to be King!"

Nascus kicked with what strength he could summon and looked in desperation to the General for aid. But Fragit's struggle had ceased. He was tightly wound in the snake's coil, its cruel fangs sunk deep into his neck.

Sintus brought his beak down in a rush, and, pecking into Nascus's eye, ripped it from the socket in victory. Nascus screamed in agony beneath him.

FROM WITHIN THE trees around and the lines above the doves watched, but they did not fight. They only whispered to one another. And every few moments one whispered into another's ear and took off in what seemed some random direction, then another would land in its place and listen to the whispers of the others.

Chapter Seventeen

Unrightful Heirs

WHEN YSIL HAD been a tiny chick, he had seen three ducks descend into the field to feed. Ducks seldom stopped here, as there was only a small stream nearby and no sufficient shelter. But they did sometimes visit when there was plentiful food. The crows were not fond of ducks but tolerated them on the seldom occasion they would visit. The two bird kinds were of near the same size, and their diets varied enough that the crows did not feel threatened. When his grandfather had seen them, he had gone to them and talked, making friendly acquaintance.

Likewise, General Fragit had come into the field and, with respect, asked the ducks to leave. Cotur Ada had a brief argument with the General. Ysil had watched from the brush, the same spot, in fact, from which he now watched the war before him. That had been the first time he had ever seen Fragit. Now he witnessed the General's death. From the first moment he had seen the General, he had disliked him intensely. Now Ysil felt a great sadness to see him dead on the ground, even though just two days prior he had watched Fragit kill his grandfather. With the General's death, Ysil knew hope was fading.

It was then that he heard a thunderous rumbling. It began as a low-pitched pounding and then became a rampant drumming. It was the beating of many heavy hooves on the forest floor. Suddenly, the sound was all around him. Then, on either side of the brush, out burst bucks, one after another. They came in a far greater number than he remembered from the grove. Some were larger with thickly branched antlers; others were smaller with short spikes jutting from their heads.

The deer raced into the field and upon the fray of battle. Instinctively, some of the foxes ran. But Ysil saw that they did not run far. The lead deer was Illanis, and he plowed headlong into a group of coyotes. With his tremendous antlered head, he hoisted the lot of them into the air with ease, impaling one of their number. Most of them flew to the ground and ran. The impaled coyote he shook off and began to maul with his hooves.

Now there were the scurrying forms of squirrels racing into the field. They were into the battle immediately, biting the weasels and minks with their formidable teeth. The weasels were vicious, however, and fought back with wrath. Harlequin pressed tightly to Ysil as one of the weasels ripped a squirrel's neck open with its tiny, ferocious fangs.

There was a beating of wings overhead, and Ysil saw the shape of a giant black bird settle in the tree above. Ysil looked around the field and saw that when the crows had flown into battle, the vultures had taken their places in the surrounding trees. They were gathered in anticipation for a feast, one that was quickly being laid out below them.

ASMOD MADE HIS killings count. Those he attacked were the largest and most challenging of their kind. He had used this tact, when on the hunt, to keep a herd of deer always without a strong, aged leader. Now was the same. This had never been the way of the pack, which would take the weakest, the young or the old. But when hunting alone, it had to be this way. Take out the leader and send the rest into chaos.

He saw the two princes fighting viciously, and noted Sintus tearing the eye from the other's head. Prone on the ground was the crow he took to be the General of the army. Tortrix slithered off the poisoned corpse. *This is going exceptionally well*, he thought.

Then he heard the pounding of the hooves. He noted the alpha deer immediately, and as the antlered males tore through the coyotes, sending them sprawling and running, he moved to the great buck's rear. Close at his side were the two foxes he had just allowed to join his army. Up to this point in the battle, the two had stayed near him, forcing off attacks from his rear. Now they joined him without command as he approached the deer.

The deer jumped quickly, seeing the movement approaching from behind, and swung his huge head toward Asmod.

"Curse you, wolf!" cried the deer. "I will send you to hunt with the packs in hell!" And with that he lowered his antlers and charged Asmod.

The wolf jumped quickly but was not fast enough. The deer bore down on him with great speed and plowed into him broadside. The wolf was too large to hoist above the deer's head, but Illanis pushed him hard and fast. Asmod was impaled through the shoulder by one lengthy tine and wrestled furiously to free himself. With great pain he howled in rage. Then the foxes were on Illanis's head, tearing and thrashing at his eyes, ears, and neck. The deer snorted and huffed, struggling to get free. The tine within Asmod's shoulder pulled out, and the wolf took his chance. He rushed with open mouth to the deer's neck, clasping his sharp teeth in deep. The deer snorted and bellowed in hysterical frenzy. Another deer charged in to his aid, this one a large doe. She pounded her feet down in a maul of sharp hooves upon the wolf's head. The wolf turned and set his teeth free from the buck and jumped at the doe, biting her and tasting fresh blood, dragging her to the ground.

And then the buck was at his side again, goring him with his antlers. Asmod turned back to the deer and fought. Then with a rush of dark brown and a great roar, a fell creature pounced upon the buck. The thing bellowed in fury and ripped out one of the deer's eyes with its long and horrible claws while at the same time sinking its fangs into the buck's neck. From the bush, Ysil saw the creature attack, and though he had never seen one, he knew what it must be. It was a monster of nightmare to him: the wolverine. The deer bellowed in agony. Now he was bleeding profusely and weakening fast. Asmod looked around and saw a good many deer still fighting or standing their ground, but many turned and ran when they heard the lead buck's dying screams. There were many dead crows, squirrels, and a few young deer all about the field. The sky began to fill with fleeing crows, already admitting defeat.

As the buck grew still, Asmod smiled into the eyes of the wolverine, but the creature only glared blindly back, seeming to look past the wolf to some undetermined point beyond. When the wolverine sensed the buck was dead, it did not stay. The thing took off in a scurrying run from the continuing battle and disappeared into the forest.

A crimson river flowed freely from Asmod's shoulder and brow. Still he lusted on the rage of battle, and he fed off the pain. The blood he drank replaced that which he shed.

THROUGH THE FOGGY vision of his single eye, Nascus looked up at his brother and knew he was going to die. Sintus raised his head and readied to strike. Then there came a whoosh, and in a great rush of gray and white wings, Sintus was gone, hoisted away in a flush.

Nascus looked up to see his brother being dragged away by a great horned owl. Two crows were immediately at the owl's neck and face, pecking and scratching. The owl let loose his catch, and Sintus came tumbling down to the ground. Then the great owl was gone as fast as he had come, his gray and white form disappearing into the clouded sky.

Then Nascus made his choice. He looked one more time to his General and saw that he lay in a lifeless heap, the copperhead slithering away from his body.

When the deer came, he had felt a brief rise of hope, but now Illanis, the leader of the deer, lay dead with the wolf still tearing at his neck. He saw the doe Oda running for the forest now, the flash of a tiny yellow bird at her side. All the deer were fleeing, as were the squirrels that were still alive. Some of the crows who were there to protect the field were milling about, now taking the side of the victor with no other choice but to fly.

And with that Nascus took wing, struggling to rise, fast. He flew in the direction of the rising sun and the cold wind with one last hope rising around his heart like thorns binding a locust tree.

YSIL SAW A black bird take wing from the Murder's Tree. It flew with force and purpose straight to Sintus. It was Ophrei the rook, the sage.

The bird landed screaming.

"You are not the chosen King!" he bellowed. "You will never receive the true crown! Never from me nor the wind!"

"And who are you to say who is worthy of the true crown?" It was the copperhead that asked this. From his hiding place Ysil struggled to hear its small and bilious voice. "I am no friend to the wind, and I would say that the new King Crow will receive his crown under the authority of my lord, the earth."

"A crow of the earth?" said Ophrei. "This is unheard of!"

"And who are you, may I ask?" This came from the wolf, still covered in the gore of battle, his side bleeding. He moved in on the rook, closer now.

"I am the rook, Ophrei, adviser to the King and interpreter of the wind."

"We pay the wind no heed. We care not what it may say."

The rook opened his great beak to protest, but the wolf did not give him the time to do so. Though Asmod was injured, this made him only more furious. He pounced on the rook, and with one bite, took off his head. Ophrei's dead form fell with an audible thud and after one convulsion was still.

It was then that a great gust of wind took over the field. It blew with force over the body of the sage listener. It was as if the body were only a pile of black feathers, and they all lifted up onto the wind, leaving no bones, flesh, or beak behind. And from where Ysil, Cormo, and Harlequin hid, they could see the feathers drifting high and into the sky.

The wind died and the wolf sat staunchly upon his haunches. He reared back his blood-drenched head and howled, and the coyotes and the foxes joined him. The victor crows cawed along with the beasts, gathering around Sintus and bowing low before him. And so it was the one not chosen who claimed the kingship.

And within the brush, the quail huddled in fear. All around the field mice, moles, voles, and rabbits trembled in terror, for they were too slow to flee and too small to fight.

And even as the howl of the wolf echoed through the fall wind, the vultures fell upon the field and moved among bird and predator alike. And neither beast nor crow spoke to them nor looked them in the eye as they set to their grisly task.

Chapter Eighteen

Lupus Rex

AND SO SINTUS, the King Crow, and his General, Darus, set to collecting willow boughs and branches of the slippery elm tree to build upon the nest. They gathered within the nest the skulls of the past Kings in one place. When the nest was made, Sintus took to it and sat upon high, overlooking the field.

To him came all the crows, and all confessed their allegiance, though some did not look him in the eye. Sintus was proud and knew that in time they would accept his reign. High in his nest he felt strong. He looked below and saw a young coyote nip at the tail of a crow. The bird jumped to the tree above and called down to the coyote, cursing. Hot anger welled up within his belly and moved with a rush to the crown of his head. It was clear that the field was not his at all. Though the nest was unchallenged, safe in the heights of the tree, it came on him in a rush of realization that the field now belonged only to the wolf. He had thought of the two ruling side by side, both with control of the field. Now he feared this would not be so. He shuffled in his new nest and counted the skulls of his grandfathers beneath him. His father's was still covered with black feathers, the dull eyes glazed and ivory within the sockets.

HARLEQUIN SAW HER first. The mother vulture was moving through the ranks of her kind as they tore at the bodies of the animals lying dead.

"Look, Ysil!" whispered Harlequin, fidgeting excitedly. "That's the mother vulture, the one they call Ekbeth."

Immediately the vulture glared directly at their hiding place, as if she had heard them speaking. But she was too far away to hear them. How could she know they were there? Her eyes darted briefly to the Murder's Tree and to the wolf that was licking his wounds in its shadow. Then she moved slowly in their direction.

"She's coming this way!" whispered Ysil. "Should we run? Could she mean us harm?"

"Surely no harm," said Cormo, who had been quite close to the vulture just days before. "She is somewhat kind, actually." With that, Ysil eyed him with mild shock. "Well—in her own way, that is . . ."

Ekbeth wobbled and plodded uneasily through the field, mindfully picking at the bloody grass for scraps. Before long she was at the field's edge, her wing within reach of their hiding spot.

She extended her long neck into the thicket, her yellow eyes opening wide. "Hello, little ones," she said to the quail. "And so, alas, it is up to you to make the next move, for neither crows nor deer are capable of fighting a battle at this time. They may come soon, but they may not. Of course, we vultures are not really on any side at all, as we are most certainly grateful for this feast." She stank with the oily smell of fresh blood, but beneath that was a rich, darker stench, one of old things and forgotten places.

"Next move?" asked Ysil, from within the bush. "What move could we hope to make that could influence anything at all? We are even fearful to flee, as if we do, surely the predators will know we are here." Ysil looked down at the dried, dead leaves below him and remembered his grandfather's words: *I will always be with you. . .* Could he really do something to weaken the wolf? To defeat the unworthy new King Crow?

"My dear little bird, I am afraid the wolf and his kind know very well that you are here, as I and my kind do likewise." She smiled in her own unique way. "We can smell you." She once again bounced her bald head in the direction of the Murder's Tree then quickly bounced it back and moved in a bit closer. "You are small, yes, but sometimes size is not that important. This action I suggest for you to take now will bring into play those who are even smaller than you. Size is not important if your numbers are in the thousands. I have a suggestion for you, that is all. And if truth be told, the dead are the dead to us, and we would just as soon pick the bones of the wolf as of the deer—or quail." Ysil shivered but kept looking the vulture straight in the eye. "We could always eat more. And though the plan I have for you may not bring about the death of the wolf, it will at least aggravate his wretched soul." She shuddered and an issuing of dried blood rained from her feathers. "But should you not succeed in your mission, you likely will not live to tell me of your failing."

And so Ekbeth told them of her plan, one both dangerous and possible. The quail listened and feared but found some hope. And when she had finished, she silently moved back into the field.

The three looked at one another with expectation.

"Could it really work?" asked Cormo.

"Perhaps," said Ysil. "But it is hugely treacherous!"

"Ysil," said Harlequin, "we should do this thing. We owe it to Gomor and Cotur Ada and the others who have died at least to try."

Ysil and Cormo stared back at her for a moment, then at each other.

"Yes," said Ysil. "We must try, at least."

They crept away from their hiding place until they felt at a safe distance. Then they took to the air, flying with all the force their wings could muster, over the golden and red treetops, past the man's house, and on to a sizable stand of pine beyond. They flew to the tallest of the pines, gnarled and old, and landed upon its upper branches. With undeniable danger hanging just below them, they looked at the immense, pasty nest and considered their next move.

TORTRIX LAY AT his King's side, his only King. From beneath him came a tremble, as if far, far below a great beast rolled over within the fiery center of the world. The snake laid his head to one side and listened intently for some time. Then he smelled the air with his tongue.

"I have returned to the land of my birth and taken it as my own. I will never leave again, not alive," said the wolf. Asmod was hurt, but he had stopped bleeding.

"I am with you, my King," said the copperhead. "I have a word from the earth for you."

"A word from the earth?" asked Asmod, uncertain.

"Yesss. As the rook hears the words of the wind, I likewise hear the speakings of the earth. The earth is in agreement with you. It sssayss you are to be the only king here. It sssayss that the crows are not itss own and should not consider the field theirs likewise."

"Yes, this I know to be true. I have felt it also." Asmod rose. "You are to be the sage of the field, Tortrix," said the wolf. "You are the interpreter of the earth and closest to it of all."

"And sssurely you are the only King—"

"Treachery!" came a scream from the branches above. "You speak treachery!" It was Darus, the General of all the murder, that screamed now; he had been spying on their whisperings.

Then Sintus was there, at Darus's side.

"What is this treachery you speak of, Darus?"

The wolf and snake glared up. Around them were Drac and Puk, and moving in were three coyotes and another fox. Many weasels and lizards were killed in battle, but still there were some left, and they also moved closer to the wolf.

"He speaks of the fact that I am the only true King here," asserted the wolf.

The crows above began to gather in the branches with Sintus. They all looked to their leader for some action or command, though their reaction to such would be less than enthusiastic. Sintus stared at the wolf in shock.

"You may have your tree and your new nest, but as you can see," said the wolf, looking around at his followers, "we hold the field."

"Traitor!" screamed Sintus. "We were to rule both the field and the Murder's Tree together."

"Well, perhaps you will descend and we can come to a conclusion on that down here." Asmod looked at Tortrix. "Down to earth, we might say, eh, Tortrix?"

And with that the wolf began to laugh, and his laugh turned into the challenge of a bitter howl.

Sintus cawed in rueful fury and flew back to his nest. Darus and all of his army gathered close to consider what to do about the wolf and its band below. About the nest, the skulls of his grandfathers and father stared at him with vacant, disdainful eyes. And below the nest, posted unnoticed upon the tip of a dead branch, the tiny skull of Cotur Ada viewed the beasts below, his gaze equally void.

Asmod walked from underneath the tree and out into the field. "My followers! We are victorious!" A rousing hurray came in response. "But alas, we are yet to dispose of our final enemy! I speak of the crows in the tree above!"

Howls and yelps of agreement came back.

"And to each of you, snakes and lizards alike. When you sleep in the winter's cold, the crows will surely rout your nests and tear you up!"

To this there were sounds of agreement, a chorus of hisses. And as the hisses settled, before the wolf could go on, there came a steady and growing buzz. Asmod stopped and looked toward the sound.

Out of the tree line burst a small quail, flying with hasty speed straight at the wolf and his army. The wolf laughed.

"What is this? Has this quail decided to fight me? Perhaps a brave little suicide?" Around him the other animals laughed as the quail grew closer.

Then the source of the buzz came into sight in the form of a great yellow cloud, churning and enraged. The cloud was moving in a swift, roiling motion across the field.

The quail was fleeing these hornets, not attacking. And as the wolf realized this, it came to him that perhaps the quail was not fleeing randomly, and was in fact leading the hornets precisely where he intended.

After the tiny quail raced past, inches above the wolf's head, it became clear what the bird was doing. It dived headlong into the freshly cut grass, putting the wolf between itself and the attacking hornets.

"Clever little bird. . ." Asmod mumbled. But it was too late to do anything. The hornets were upon him.

NO ONE EVER spoke to the hornets. They would not listen. The hornets kept to themselves and tended to their own and seldom sought anyone out, unless that someone could be eaten. No one approached a hornet. If a hornet came close to one, buzzing and irritated (as hornets always are), one gently backed away. No one spoke to the hornets.

The first memory Ysil had of hornets was when Cotur Ada warned Cormo and him against them. But his grandfather had taken them near the nest, so they would know the hornets' borders and range. Cotur Ada had flown in close to the pine grove and, from the edge of it, on a cool, late spring day while the hornets were sleeping (they hoped), he had pointed out the nest. It was hanging from a lower branch, arcane and wondrous, the color of birch bark. But when Ysil asked if it was a part of the tree, his grandfather said no, that the hornets made it with their spit.

"Their spit?" said Ysil.

"That's disgusting," said Cormo. "You mean they live in a house made of their own spit?"

"That is exactly where they live," said Cotur Ada. "And they are especially proud of their home. Never touch it. Never even get near it. If you do, they may all come out in a rush and sting you at once. This would kill you. We have a rule with the hornets, one we never break: leave them alone, and they will leave us alone. This is within the order."

And when Ysil, Harlequin, and Cormo had perched above the hornets' nest, they heard the buzzing within. But there were no hornets to be seen around the grove.

"I'll do it," said Cormo.

"I must be the one," said Ysil. "Cormo, you and I race all the time." He looked at Harlequin, not wanting to sound like he was bragging. "Who wins, Cormo?"

Cormo stared back. "You do," he said.

"Be careful," said Harlequin.

"There is nothing careful, nor sane for that matter, about what I am going to do, not at all," said Ysil, and the three shared a brief, nervous laugh.

Ysil flew down upon the branch the nest was welded to and moved carefully and quietly toward it. There were still no hornets to be seen, only the steady buzz from within. He knew this was a dire measure, but he must do something to stop the wolf, even if it meant his own death. Then he did exactly what Ekbeth had suggested. He poked a hole in the nest with his beak, one quick and strong peck, and with all the strength his wings could propel, he flew back in the direction of the field, and he did not look back. Before he cleared the edge of the pine grove, he heard the buzzing din of angry hornets pursuing him.

And so he led the angry mob to the field, and once again, as he flew, there at the tip of his wing, just for an instant, he was sure he had seen another bird flying with him.

THE HORNETS WERE about the wolf like a funnel cloud, and immediately engulfed his body. Asmod howled in pain and began to thrash about, biting and pawing at the angry insects. Those close to him were caught in the cloud also. Tortrix was stung and slithered away fast, dragging one writhing hornet with him, its stinger impaled deeply in the snake's rust-colored back. And then the wolf was rolling across the ground, smashing hornets beneath him and wailing in agony. The hornets then left the wolf and flew onto a young coyote close by. They covered the coyote in a writhing yellow blanket. The coyote struggled and twisted its body, biting at its hide. And then the hornets were on a nearby fox, leaving the coyote wriggling about in a poisoned daze.

Ysil lay motionless on the field in the midst of this mayhem, hoping that for another moment he would go unnoticed in the chaos. He was exhausted, his eyes nearly swollen shut. Perhaps he would appear a small brown stone in the great field, but alas, his quick breathing would give him away. The wolf stood up and looked around. Ysil knew that if he were to flee, it must be now. So he jumped to the air and flew with all his might.

"After the little bird!" screamed Asmod. "Bring him to me!"

But Ysil did not look back. He was nearly at the edge of the field now. Safety was only a few feet away. Closer... Closer...

Then with a red blur before him, he was brought to the ground. He felt the teeth tight in his side, and beneath that spot he felt and heard the tight snap and crunch of a rib bone breaking. He looked around frantically to see who his captor was and saw the smiling eyes of Drac—and a swift movement to his left was Puk. Puk had something in his mouth also: the struggling form of Harlequin.

"Bring them to me!" bellowed Asmod from the center of the field.

CORMO AND HARLEQUIN had followed just behind the swarm and taken to the edge of the field. They watched in wonder as the hornets overwhelmed the huge wolf. They had seen the wolf's struggles and saw their friend take flight toward them. No sooner had Ysil jumped than a great thrashing occurred in the brush behind them. They both flushed quickly, but Harlequin had not been fast enough. Cormo looked back to see her taken to the ground by the familiar form of the scoundrel fox, Puk by name.

And with fear in his heart and tears in his eyes, Cormo had taken high into the air and flown away fast, the terror of his own death propelling him forward, close at his tail feathers.

He had flown only a short distance before he realized what he was doing: fleeing and leaving his friends to die. With a fresh resolve he came down and landed within the high branches of a sycamore. He looked back to the field.

There at its edge were the shapes of two red foxes, and within their jaws were the twisting and thrashing forms of two little gray birds.

NO SOONER HAD the hornets come than they were gone, the cloud moving with its raging purpose back in the direction from where it had come, a bit smaller now than upon its arrival.

Asmod was lying on his side, stung all over. Still, he was crazed with wrath. He heard laughter from above and looked up. Sintus was just above him, circling low with five other crows. "So, the tiniest of the enemies has caused the great wolf the most pain!" said Sintus.

"I am in need of a truce, as certainly we do need each other!" said Asmod. His face was beginning to swell, as was the back of his neck and his posterior. Tortrix gingerly slithered back to his side, the tip of his tail stretched to twice its normal size, an enormous hornet stinger protruding from it.

Drac and Puk were to the wolf now, and they laid Ysil and Harlequin down, holding them firmly with their paws. Ysil's side throbbed in agony. Harlequin was awake but seemed in shock. Ysil looked to her but she did not look back, though her eyes were wide open. They were both trembling all over.

"You cursed little birds," Asmod said. "You will die long, painful deaths for this." He looked up and forced his puffy body to stand. "Hear me! Hear me, all who are in hiding about the field! I know you are all there! I can smell every one of you. Let the deaths of these two be a warning memory to you, lest we kill you all as you sleep in the night or gather during the day! I am the King of this field!" And he looked at Sintus. "Beside Sintus I will rule!" Tortrix looked up to the wolf and tongued the air.

Circling above, the new King Crow heard the words of the wolf and wondered. Certainly, Asmod could not be trusted—not ever, but he was injured now. Perhaps this attack by the hornets had stirred an awareness of his need to keep allegiance with the crows. Surely the wolf was in need now. Sintus made his decision and flew down beside the wolf. "I am glad you have come to clear mind, wolf. Too bad it took the stings of a thousand hornets and the betrayal of a mere quail to bring you to your senses."

"Oh, yes," said Asmod. "My senses are quite awake. In fact, I never lost them."

And with that, he reared up and was on Sintus in a flash, grabbing the big black bird within his jaws. Then Darus and another were on the wolf, trying to fight him away, but it was too late. Asmod tore the newly crowned King Crow's chest apart, casting his ravaged form to the ground. And so it was that finally Sintus's salty blood poured down upon the earth, and the field ate it up greedily.

As Ysil watched Sintus die, he felt all hope die with him. Within the crow's order there had always been a place for the quail, rabbits, and other lower animals, and though he remembered what Cormo had heard from his perch above the trail, that being Sintus's agreeing to the deaths of all quail, with the crows, at least there was some hope.

Within the order of the wolf, there was none at all. The remainder of the crows gathered about and bowed low and professed Asmod the only King, of the field and also the Murder's Tree.

The wolf once again turned his puffy head high and howled in victory. The others joined in. And as the yelps and howls of the predators died out, the cry of victory turned into a defiant screech. It came from above, a sound that spoke deep within Ysil's heart. It was a sound that brought new fear, but for some reason, also hope. Ysil looked to the left and saw the shape of the wolverine move into the field. The darkly furred monster was looking up into the sky; he shook his head and turned quickly away. As the wolverine disappeared into the dark woods from where it had come, the screech continued, becoming louder each second, the whole of the field growing deathly quiet. Ysil looked up, and there, high in the sky, were the forms of birds. The shapes grew larger as they descended with great speed. The first bird was much larger than the other shapes behind it: brown, with the tips of his wings gray and bearing white highlights across. And it was a bird he knew.

"Pitrin," he heard in a whisper. It was Harlequin. "It is Pitrin, returned at last."

Chapter Nineteen

The Final Battle

DAY'S LIGHT WAS fading and dark would soon come, relentless and unavoidable. All eyes, those within the field and those around it, were upon the sky. Now the shapes of the birds were clear upon the gray backdrop of racing cloud. It was the great hawk returned, and behind him was the one-eyed prince of the crows: the chosen Nascus. And the wind blew straight down from the heavens and dropped them with a fury.

So concerned were they with the descending birds, none of the predators heard the approaching attack from the forest. Out of four corners of the field burst four groups of animals. One, from the direction of the cold wind, was the remainder of the deer, led by Oda, the widow, injured but racing into battle. Flying at her side was the tiny form of Flax, scarcely larger than a hornet himself. From the direction of the setting sun came an army of turkeys with Butry in lead. From the direction of the rising sun charged the remainder of the squirrels and a pack of badgers. Within this number was Risa the woodchuck, racing ahead of the others with fangs bared. And from the direction of the warm wind came the greatest gathering of raccoons ever assembled, and all sprinted toward the wolf and his band at once.

The predators panicked, surrounded from all sides and from above. They all packed in together, huddled up against Asmod.

The wolf screamed, "In rank! Prepare for battle!" Tortrix wrapped around the wolf's neck in protection and for safety.

Drac and Puk loosened their paws from Ysil and Harlequin. The quail burst free, taking fast to wing. Ysil was in great pain, but he paid it no mind. The two birds flew tight together, straight over the top of the turkeys, which ran, hopped, and flew into battle.

The two small birds flew straight to their hiding place and watched in anticipation. There was a rustle beside them and up looked Cormo, a great relief in his eyes.

Before them, the deer were upon the predators, crashing in with their hooves and antlers, some of them wounded. Fueled by the hope of victory and revenge, they fought even stronger than before. A coyote's skull was cracked, his head dashed upon the sharp end of a hoof. Puk ran. He raced for what he thought was a break in the pounding hooves, but just as he broke past two attacking deer, Oda was upon him. She beat him to death with her flogging legs. Drac tried to flee, only to be attacked by three raccoons at once, who tore his throat apart, singing their joyous song as they did so. A familiar coon looked Drac in the eye as he died. "We fight only when cornered, eh?" said the masked animal.

The turkeys flew upon Asmod all at once, and he thrashed and fought, tearing them up with his sharp teeth. Butry, the tom, was killed by the wolf with one quick shake of its head, the monstrous jaws clenched about his frail neck. Then the raccoons were also upon him. One of them ripped the snake from about his neck with its sharp teeth, the copperhead falling to the ground. Asmod was upon the raccoons, tearing and biting them, and one after the other he was killing them. They screamed and barked, their blood flying into the air. Still they attacked him, one after another, and with each he would dispatch, Asmod was pounced upon by another. But the wolf would not go down, and he was killing the assailants as fast as they came at him.

Asmod reared up on his hind legs to wail a victory cry to frighten those attacking. The tastes of raccoon's and turkey's blood were strong in his mouth. The wolf heard only one beat of a wing, and he did not have time to register what it might be before the hawk was upon him. With deft purpose and aim, Pitrin jabbed his beak into the wolf's head and plucked out his remaining eye. The wolf's howl of victory became one of agony. Pitrin did not even slow, but swallowed the eye down and banked sharply to return for the kill.

Asmod screamed, jumping about wildly.

Pitrin bore down upon the great wolf, his talons outstretched, his red beak open in attack. The wolf thrashed madly about, biting at the air, yelping and howling. But when the hawk was nearly upon him, Tortrix burst like a bolt into the air. Pitrin banked sharply to avoid the deadly fangs of the snake. There came another beat of wings and, suddenly, Strix the owl took the snake in midflight; he flew far and high with the snake, who would not return living to the earth.

By this time dusk was upon the field, and with the dying light Ysil saw the great bleeding and blind wolf burst from the middle of battle and race in the direction of the falling sun. Asmod, the last wolf, blinded and wounded, disappeared with a rustle into the forest, none in pursuit. Pitrin flew in a tight arc around the foray, quickly returning to where the wolf had been, but found the beast had disappeared.

Still the battle raged, but not for long. The predators became aware that their leader was no longer in the field and began to flee: limping, howling, barking, and seething. Across the field were the bodies of the dead. As the sounds of battle died, and the moans of the injured calmed or ended, twilight fell. The clouds billowed across the gray sky, and the light of day was swallowed by a whole and complete darkness. Ysil heard no screams of victory, just the milling of deer and raccoons, and of course the tearing of the vultures. The wind quieted and all grew still.

As Ysil, Cormo, and Harlequin settled into the inevitable sleep of quail, Ysil heard from upon high, as if from an approaching dream, the lone screech of Pitrin, returned to the nest of his birth.

Chapter Twenty

The Claims of the Brother

WITH THE DAWN came a drenching rain, and the water rinsed the field, cleansing and purifying. Blood of both predator and prey, bird and innocent, washed down into the thirsty earth. And with the rain came the promise of fall, days ever colder and longer nights.

Ysil and Harlequin woke to the sound of the falling rain, and for the hours it fell they did not move but lay there within the brush and talked quietly among themselves. Finally the light of the sun folded across the field, and there returned to collect the bounty of the dead those whose right is so.

"Is it really over?" asked Harlequin.

"Certainly it must be," said Cormo. "The wolf surely died in the night."

"I feel positive also that it is over," said Ysil.

But the three sat at the edge of the field, still within the brush, and watched as the vultures tended to the dead.

Nascus, the new King Crow, descended upon the field and talked with the vultures, with Ekbeth and the others. And all was still except for the sound of the vultures' feeding. At the edge of the field Ysil saw the movement of mice and also a small quail.

"It's Sylvil," said Harlequin. "For her to be out, she must sense all is safe."

And with so many of the lesser animals feeding, the quail made up their minds to join them, and they stepped from the brush.

Cormo went first, approaching Sylvil carefully. Cormo picked through what was there, Sylvil looking up at him shyly as he drew close. Ysil and Harlequin moved together near them, and Roe was there, munching at a rattlesnake body. Harlequin looked at him disgustedly. He smiled back a crimson grin in response. The warmth of the early fall day arrived, and the sun shone upon the field, a thick steam rising from it. And so the quail meandered about the edge of the field, picking the drying grain.

Ysil ate the grain. There arose a breeze, and though it was slight, it pressed persistently into his face. There came to his ear a whistle within the wind. He closed his eyes, listening carefully. A melody unfolded from the blowing, a rising and falling cadence, not unlike the dance of the raccoons. But the song was urgent, determined. All around Ysil the sounds of feeding disappeared, and for that moment all was erased; the loss was gone, the pain in his side forgotten. The melody surrounded him, swallowed him, and demanded his attention. It was then it became clear there was a word within the song, a word not spoken but whistled through the leaves of the trees and the cut blades of grass, and he listened, trying to determine the speaking. The word was of two tones, one higher and the second low, repeating over and over.

Abruptly, Ysil understood. His eyes burst open and the message from the wind came flying from his beak. "Warning!" he screamed.

Suddenly a horrendous gray form, stinking and bloody, jumped blindly at the small group of feeding animals. The wolf! He yelped, frenzied, snapping his bloody teeth at the birds he could smell very well, though he could not see them at all. Harlequin was close to the wolf, too close. Asmod thrashed his head harshly and the small form of Harlequin thudded to the ground, pummeled by the wolf's murderous jaws.

With the instinct of protection in him, the agonizing pain of his broken rib forgotten, Ysil jumped upon the great wolf's head and, driving down with all his might, pushed his beak into the freshly emptied socket in the wolf's skull. Asmod howled in pain. The animals at the edges of the field jumped and ran to hiding. The crows flew from the Murder's Tree, racing toward the fray. The wolf shook his head furiously, tossing off Ysil and running fast into the field, but blindly. The crows were closer now.

The wind blew strong now, and with it the rising crescendo of a chorus of whistles—a song of fury. The wolf ran. The song ended with a deafening sound like none Ysil had ever heard, except when lightning crashed down upon the ground very close. The tiny quail lay unmoving on the field's silage. The crows broke their descent and scattered. There, only a few feet away, stood the man, a long stick smoking in his hand. The immense wolf was lying limp on the field. The wind had dropped to a dead calm.

* * *

HARLEQUIN WAS LYING beside the wolf. The man walked up to the gigantic gory form and kicked the dead beast, making a grunt of sorts as he watched it for a moment, then kicked it again. He paid no attention to the insignificant quail, as if he had not even perceived their presence. Satisfied, he reached down and took Asmod by the leg and, with some effort, dragged him to the edge of the field and out of sight.

Ysil went to her. "Harlequin, are you all right?"

For one horrifying moment Ysil thought her dead. She lay so still, eyes shut tight. Then Harlequin stirred. "What was that?"

"That was the end of the wolf," answered Ysil. She pressed her head to his outstretched wing.

Then with a great gust Pitrin settled down nearby, and beside him landed Nascus and the other crows.

"You are brave, little quail," said Nascus. "The murder has told me of your courageous flight with the hornets at your back. It was you who turned the tide of the battle. I had my spies within the tree as I sought out Pitrin. And now," Nascus said, laughing a bit at this, "as the blind wolf attacked your friend, your tiny beak sent him screaming."

"He is brave, certainly," said Pitrin. "And he is my brother." The hawk pulled Cotur Ada's feather from his breast, laying it at the feet of Ysil. The crows looked at him in shock, but Nascus made no sign of surprise, his eyes sparkling.

Ysil looked up at the noble hawk in wonder. The massive bird took to wing, bearing his form high to his nest, and there he settled, disappearing into the tangle of branches.

* * *

THE NEXT DAY Ysil went to the Murder's Tree unannounced, and with him he brought the feather of Cotur Ada. Nascus was tending to the nest and had set the skulls in a row at its back. His father and father's father watched, eyeless, as the quail settled into the nest.

Nascus looked up and smiled with amused astonishment.

"Well, little quail, you are a brave one," he said. "I would say this is the first time a quail has ever set foot within this nest. To what do I owe the honor of your visit?"

Ysil was nervous, but within his heart he held a purpose that urged him on.

"I bring you this feather, King," said Ysil. "I bring it to you in the hopes you will keep it in your nest. Keep it near, lest you forget the wisdom of my grandfather. For he warned of the wolf, but none would listen."

Nascus smiled, and with that smile Ysil decided that Nascus would be a wise King. "I will keep it, little quail. I will always remember."

The King Crow tucked the feather within his nest, then he reached down, and very carefully picked up a small thing. He pressed this thing into a space beside the skulls of the dead King Crows and stepped back. It was Cotur Ada's tiny skull, in line beside Mellori's.

Ysil stammered and cried, and he flew from the nest.

Behind him Nascus called out one last time, "I will always remember!"

* * *

YSIL WENT BACK to the brush where he was born. And there were Harlequin and Cormo. As the day wore on, Ysil felt within him the gathering of a new order. And the nest in which he rested felt safer than before. As night descended once again on Murder's Field and those who lived within and near it, Ysil and Harlequin nuzzled up to each other and slept the sleep of the free.

Epilogue

THE WINTER CAME fast that season, ripping the leaves from the trees like a starving bear stripping a sapling. The pale blanket of snow draped across the field and the woods, confining the hibernating animals comfortably within their dens—the mice, woodchucks, and moles huddled together in a blissful, cozy sleep. The snow that had fallen during the night, as the moon above lit the clouded sky from horizon to horizon, continued to fall into the first hours of day. The grain was beneath the snow, and most animals that did not hibernate or go south were taken to eating from that which was stored away, or the rare dug hickory nut or an acorn pilfered from an empty den. And though the sun peeked through the occasional break in the clouds, the chill was deep and bitter that morning.

Ysil peered out from the brush and into the field as the fourth hour of day's light crept toward the fifth. He watched as King Nascus flew in tight circles around the tree, with each revolution taking on more black screeching birds in his wake. Around the tree a thick cloud of crows developed.

This was the wedding of the crows, and Cotur Ensis—now the eldest of the quail and successor to Cotur Mono—had told Ysil the day before to rise early and watch the wedding and departure. This was the time of year when the birds took mates and together, in pairs or in groups, left for Miscwa Tabik-kizi. Ensis had told Ysil the day of preparation for his eldership was at hand, that he would soon become Cotur Ysil. He wanted Ysil to see all he could in the next season, for Ysil had been chosen to one day become the leader of the quail.

In their circular flight the crows squawked and screamed in seeming chaos until finally Nascus went silent, and with him, all the rest of the birds. The sun shone brightly for the moment, and the crows made one last circle about the great tree, then embarked as a great mass to the north, with King Nascus in the lead.

Ysil watched the crow's departure, the sound of their wings softening as they got farther away. Then settled a complete stillness over the snowy field, and with it came the force of a great sadness within Ysil's heart. He thought of all that had come and gone in the past few moons. He thought of his grandfather, of watching him die. He thought of the loss of one of his dearest friends to the same creature who would eventually become his final savior. Was it worth the cost? And he thought of Harlequin, likely upon their nest now, feeling the steady beat of the hearts beneath her warm belly within the six eggs she kept. She was nesting early, but Ysil had a great hope for the chicks beneath her breast. The strength of their ancestors' blood was strong.

With the thought of Harlequin and the eggs, he turned to go back to their nest. But without warning there came a great swoop of wings. *The hawk!* With fearful instinct, Ysil almost flushed, but his fear was subdued, seeing as the last time he had been in his presence, the hawk had called him brother.

But then he looked up, and his fear returned with a force. It was not the form of a hawk that was upon him, but the rare sunlit body of the great owl. Ysil froze in place with a great shock, and, as the bird bore down on him, he only had time to think to himself, *This must be how the owl gets his prey; he freezes them in fear.*

Then the bird was upon him. Ysil fainted dead away.

YSIL WOKE AND opened his eyes, and there just above him was the great beak of the owl, its very tongue red and so close he could smell the decay on its breath.

"Well, hello, little bird," said Strix. "And so we meet at last."

HARLEQUIN SAT IN the nest, the round forms of the eggs beneath her reassuring and comforting. She had worried about Ysil when he left that morning and even asked him to stay, uncertain why she was concerned.

"All is fine," he told her. "I'll be back with a sprig of hackberries for you. I saw some yesterday near the rabbits' dens." He had smiled at her and nuzzled her neck warmly. She had smiled back, but since he left an uneasiness had settled on her like the powdery snow.

There came a flutter from the bush. She looked up in hopeful expectation. Then came another rustle and out stepped Cormo.

"Oh, I was hoping you were Ysil," said Harlequin.

"Well," he said with a smirk, "fine greeting for an old friend. Where *is* Ysil, by the way?"

"Cotur Ensis suggested he go watch the crows' wedding and their departure, but I would have thought he would be back by now."

"Well, I suppose I could go look for him," said Cormo. "Did he say he was going to watch from the near corner of the field? He's been foraging there a good bit lately."

"I don't think he was going that far," she said. "He said he would be back quick—as soon as the crows left—so he should be close."

"I'll go look for him." And with that Cormo took off to the brush.

The wind settled and the snow continued. Harlequin chilled a bit within the nest and settled down, her colors mixing perfectly with the grays and browns of the sleeping woods around her.

Then there came a quick rush of wind, and in a flash Ysil flew in and landed with a thud in the nest.

Though Harlequin was immediately relieved at the sight of her mate, she was taken aback by his appearance. He was disheveled and looked greatly shaken up.

"Are you okay?" they both asked each other at the same time.

Ysil made a nervous laugh in response and shook his head.

"I am fine," she said. "But you, my love, are not."

"No, no, I am perfectly fine also," he said, still shaking his head. He seemed in a bit of a shock.

"You know," he said, "when my grandfather left Monroth and me in the brush and confronted Banka, he told me something. He said, 'You may find friends in unexpected places and with unsuspected faces . . . Take care whom you trust, as well as whom you do not.' I didn't know what he meant then, but now I do."

"What are you talking about, Ysil?"

"It seems that when we were upon our journey, we had a guardian watching over us. I have just been paid a visit by Strix the owl."

"Strix!" answered Harlequin in surprise. "Did he try to eat you? How did you get away?"

Ysil laughed. "How, indeed. It seems he was a friend of my grandfather's. When we first heard of old King Crow Mellori's death, Cotur Ada disappeared. He went to confer with Strix. He asked the owl to watch over the Reckoning while he was gone, and if it turned out badly, as Cotur Ada and Strix were both sure it would, the two planned to go to the hawk's land to beg his return. When Cotur Ada died, he continued his charge and kept watch over Monroth and myself. He was even watching you when you found Cormo and Gomor. He saw the foxes sneaking through the woods to your bedding site beside the dead tree that night. He was rushing in to warn you when I flew in like a fool."

"My *brave* fool!" said Harlequin.

"That night he listened to the foxes plan and decided to watch from on high. He followed us on our whole journey, but he waited on the bank of the river when we reached the hawk's land."

"This is so much to take in!" said Harlequin. "So we have a friend in the owl?"

"Well, that is why he came to me, you see." Ysil was stammering a bit. "He came to tell of his past friendship and that he is relinquishing his commitment. He has been watching us closely for a while and has decided his hunger and his charge are beginning to interfere. He came to suggest that we change our nesting place."

"Goodness! For what reason?"

"He said he feels he knows us very well now, and sees we are much like my grandfather. It seems that Cotur Ada pulled him from a nest as a chick when the wind had blown it from the tree. All the other chicks died. My grandfather had a rare and unusual love for all creatures, killer and prey alike. Strix said he had an understanding of the true order, far beyond that of the crows, quail, or his own for that matter. *The true order*. That's what the owl said. Then he said that though he has learned to love us from watching us on high, there will come a night when he will awaken in the cold winter months to come and his hunger will drive him to our nest. He came to me of himself. What say you, my love? I feel we must leave."

Harlequin sat for a long time, taking this all in. The snow was beginning to slow, but the winter's silence was still deafening. Ysil did not speak, but waited for her to go through the process of making a decision on her own.

Finally, she replied: "Wherever you are, that is where I will nest. As you lead, I will follow. Let's go away from here. We will never return. We will begin anew and form our own covey. But how will we move the eggs?"

"I can help with that," came the voice of Cormo from the brush.

Harlequin and Ysil both looked up quickly. "So you've been listening, eh?" said Harlequin.

"Just checking in on my friends," said Cormo, and behind him moved the form of another quail. It was Sylvil.

"We can help," said the meek bird. She looked at Cormo with a great love, then back to Ysil and Harlequin. "We will both go with you."

Without another word, Harlequin and Sylvil each took an egg, with Cormo and Ysil taking two, and tucked them carefully under their wings near to their bodies, and with the quiet of the snow around them, they made their way down the path that led away from the field and to the south.

And high in a pale sycamore, within the heights of the top branches, a great white bird watched them depart. When they were gone down the path, and their small forms disappeared beneath the folds of gray branches and clumps of snow, the owl took wing and flew in the opposite direction, back to a corner of the field, where he made his new nest within the sheltering green branches of the hemlock.

Acknowledgements

DUE THANKS I offer to those who read this tale and gave invaluable feedback.

First to my wife Laura Cash: thank you for sticking with me through this process.

And then to Jonathan Oliver and everyone at Ravenstone and to my agent Shawna Morey with Folio Literary Management. To Lou Robin, who has been in my life since my birth.

I offer humble gratitude to Kate Etue, Carolyn Gibney and Deborah Wiseman. And special thanks to John Francis, Lauren Moore, Shane Ownby, Douglas Smith, Josh Havill, Rick Richter, Mark Steilper, Don Cusic, Conn Hamlett, Mike Lacey, and my son Joseph Cash who all made important contributions to this book.

Also to my children Annabelle and Jack—within your hearts anything is possible. I am willing to follow.

And thanks to the Tunkhannock, Pennsylvania Public Library, The Weeping Willow Inn, Gary And Blennie Saylor, and the Skyhaven Airport.

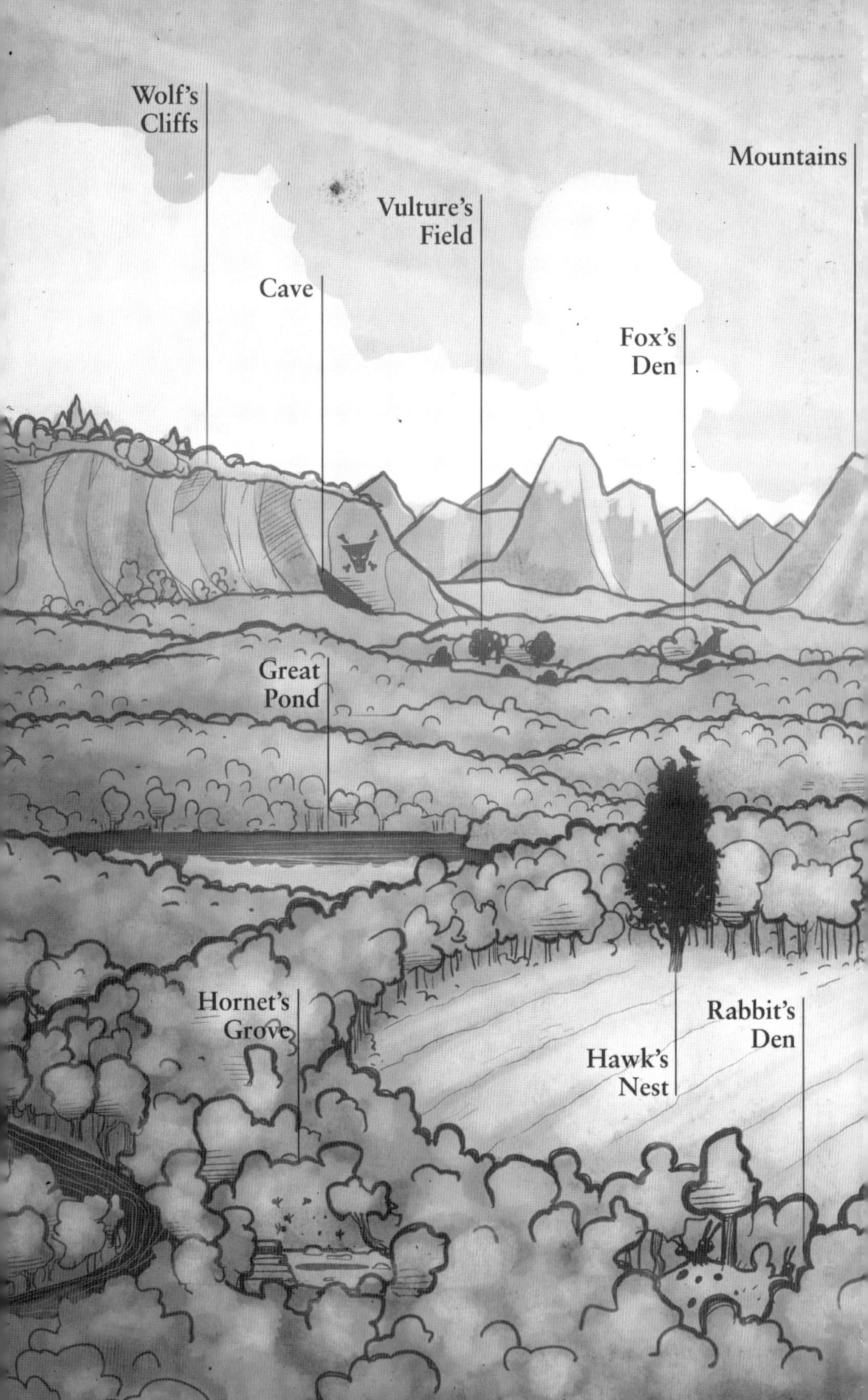
Wolf's Cliffs
Mountains
Vulture's Field
Cave
Fox's Den
Great Pond
Hornet's Grove
Rabbit's Den
Hawk's Nest